MEL BAY PRESENTS

The Complete 10-hole Diatonic Harmor

C Harmoni
Book

By James Major

**Your Reference
Guide to Available …**

- **Notes**
- **Scales**
- **Modes**
- **Positions**
- **Chords**
- **Arpeggios**
- **Bends**
- **Overbends**
- **Blues Basics**
- **Theory**
- **Diatonic Models**
- **More…**

*In Memory of:
Stanley Major, who played "Oh Susanna"
with more enthusiasm than anyone I've ever heard and
Marcelaine Major, who always smiled and listened.*

Cover Photo: James Major. Major Harmonica Collection courtesy of the Harmonica Museum of America.
www.harmonicamuseum.com

1 2 3 4 5 6 7 8 9 0

Visit us on the Web at www.melbay.com — E-mail us at email@melbay.com

Table of Contents

I would like to thank Jim Mead, the Guitarski guys and Chris Proctor for their inspiration. And also Pat Terry, Kim Driggs, Peter Choles, Hardin Davis, Bill Bay, Rick Epping, Ron Mileur, Eric Sopanen, Anna Lee, Henry Wolking, Steve Roens, Terri Major, Tracey Major, Tom Stetich, Keven Johansen, Connell Crook, Angie Keen, Sheila Van Frank and Brian Perry for their contributions. Without their help this series would not be possible.

Introduction

This book is written for beginning, intermediate and advanced players in an easy-to-use format for both music readers and non-readers. It's a quick reference guide to easily accessible notes, bends, positions, modes, chords, arpeggios and scales for any 10-hole major diatonic harmonica in the key of C. Also included is information on the more elusive overblow and overdraw notes.

The *Complete 10-hole Major Diatonic Harmonica Series* will help you understand basic music fundamentals and the vast musical capabilities of this handy little instrument in every key.

Beginning Players: Use the graphics to find any of the available chords, arpeggios, scales, modes or positions without reading music or bending a note. Basic playing techniques are also shown.

Intermediate Players: Bend your way through the available arpeggios, modes and scales. Learn how to play blues scales in seven different keys on your C harp.

Advanced Players: Learn the chromatic capabilities of a C harp. Utilize bending and overbending to play major scales in every key and refer to the theory sections to construct other needed arpeggios and scales.

Music Readers: Learn how to apply your knowledge of written music to the harmonica. See how it all fits.

Non-reading Players: Relate your knowledge of the harmonica to the graphics and expand your musical foundation. Learn new positions and arpeggios.

Use the bending chart to help find the intervals needed when mimicking string bending on an electric guitar. Discover the location of the bend intervals that will allow you to emulate your favorite pedal steel or slide guitar riffs, violin glissando and pitch bends on woodwind or brass instruments.

In the back of the book is a section on diatonic instruments that deviate from the standard 10-hole harmonica design. These models are still diatonically organized, but each has its own unique features. Some are built for playing tremolo and others for playing octaves. There are chromatic-style models that are diatonically tuned and extended-range harmonicas with additional treble and bass notes. There is also a model that allows you to bend to nearly twice as many notes as the standard diatonic harp. Players who use these models can use all of the mode, chord and arpeggio charts. This book acts as a musical reference guide for those models and more.

One book at a time, the *Complete 10-hole Major Diatonic Harmonica Series* exposes the functional capabilities of harmonicas based on the Richter system in all 12 keys.

Whether you play today's popular music, blues, rock, country, jazz, classical, folk or, for that matter, any style, applying the information in this series will improve your overall knowledge of music as it relates to the major diatonic harmonica.

Now, play through each of the examples at your own level and enjoy getting the most out of your C harp.

About the Author

Multi-instrumentalist James Major hails from suburban Detroit and started playing harmonica in 1966. In 1974 he founded the music education and lesson program at Acoustic Music in Salt Lake City. He later attended the Jazz Dept. at the University of Utah and in 1982 wrote the *Dulcimer Chord Encyclopedia* for Mel Bay Publications, Inc. Since then, he has written and produced several instructional music books. He's a seasoned music educator and continues to conduct seminars, individual and group lessons.

The Origin of the Harmonica

The harmonica is a member of the free reed family of musical instruments. Free reed instruments produce a tone when air passes over a reed that is fixed at one end and causes the other, unattached end to vibrate freely. The pitch is determined by characteristics in the flow of air over the reed, the shape of the reed, its length, weight, thickness, width, and its material.

As far back as 3000 BC in China, people made and played a free reed instrument that is commonly considered to be the predecessor of the harmonica—the "sheng." Historians have dated similar instruments back as far as 4500 BC, and variations on it are still played throughout the Far East. The ancient Chinese design is said to have had a shape that was modeled after the mythical phoenix. It has one hole in a main chamber to inhale and exhale through, and a single hole in each of the many individual bamboo pipes inserted into the main chamber. The air is channeled past a reed inside the bamboo when one or more holes are covered. Melodies or chords can be played. The same note sounds when you inhale and exhale. I've seen many different styles, some with as few as 10 bamboo pipes and others with as many as 17.

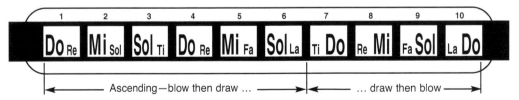

In 1295, Marco Polo's stories of the Spice Trail inspired traders to seek out goods from the Far East. They brought back many unique treasures, and in this way the free reed instrument was introduced to Europe.

During the 1770s, Pere Amiot, a Frenchman, experimented with free reed instruments by modifying the sheng in an attempt to create a new European version.

In the 1800s, a tone from a single reed, from a set of reeds, was commonly used to tune pianos and organs.

It's been widely reported that in Berlin, in 1821, Christian Friedrich Ludwig Buschmann, the son of German organmaker Johann Buschmann, invented what is considered to be the first harmonica. The then 16-year-old is said to have secured a patent for it in 1822. Buschmann put together a selection of single reeds to make a chromatic free reed instrument he called an "aura," which had all blow reeds. In 1828, the aura was described as "… a truly unique musical instrument … only four inches in diameter and equally high, with 21 notes with piano and crescendo playing possibilities, but without piano keys … with harmonies of six tones, which can be held as long as the player has breath." It was also called the "mund-aeoline," which translates from German to "mouth harp."

Martin Häffner, Director of the German Harmonica Museum in Trossinger said, "It cannot be verified at all, that the harmonica was invented in 1821 or patented in 1822. The oldest documents about harmonica makers and sellers [in Vienna] are dated 1825."

In the late 1820s, in Haidau, Bohemia, a man named Richter reinvented the instrument by putting a total of 20 reeds on two reed plates—ten on a blow plate and ten on a draw plate. He created a system of notes incorporating both an extended major scale and several chords. There are references to brothers, Josef and Anton Richter in the harmonica industry in the late 1800s, but to date, historians have been unable to find a direct link from these men to the Richter who invented the system. Some assume it may have been their father.

The Richter System Diatonic Harmonica

The configuration of intervals illustrated below is the system that was developed by Richter. The word "diatonic" refers to a seven-note scale that includes each of the notes in the musical alphabet (C, D, E, F, G, A and B.) Typically, the term "diatonic harp," when used alone, refers to the Richter-style major diatonic harmonica. There are other harmonica models made with modified diatonic tunings, such as natural minor, harmonic minor and other variations.

In this book we will be exploring the musical capabilities and boundaries of a harmonica in the key of C, using the Richter system, commonly known as the 10-hole C diatonic harmonica, or C harp.

1	2	3	4	5	6	7	8	9	10
Do Re	Mi Sol	Sol Ti	Do Re	Mi Fa	Sol La	Ti Do	Re Mi	Fa Sol	La Do

Ascending—blow then draw …   … draw then blow

Blow/draw Relationship

One notable feature of the Richter design occurs when playing ascending single notes (from left to right.) The relationship between the blow and draw notes changes in hole 7, after playing hole 6. In holes 1 through 6, you must first blow, then draw, in each hole to continue an ascending note pattern. Then, in holes 7 through 10, you must first draw and then blow, in each hole, for the ascending pattern to continue.

How To Use This Book

Hole Numbers ➤

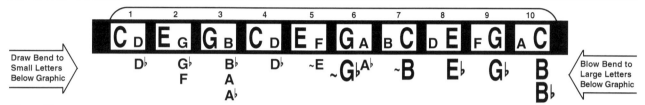

Blow and Draw Notes The graphic shows you a view of the mouthpiece of a harmonica, with the lowest notes on the left hand side and the highest notes to the right. The white squares represent the holes. The letters in the holes represent the names of the reeds or "reed notes." The larger letters represent the name of the note you hear when you exhale or "blow" air into that hole and vibrate the blow reed. The smaller letters represent the note you hear when you inhale or "draw" air through that hole and vibrate the draw reed.

Bending The letters below the harmonica represent notes you bend to and appear directly below the hole you'll use to play those notes. Draw to bend in holes 1 through 6. Blow to bend in holes 6 through 10. (See page 10.)

The hole 5 draw F note can be bent—but not all the way down to a true E note. I put it to the electronic test and the different tuners all showed that it will bend out of the F note range and into the E note range but never to a true E note. This bend can be used to add character to a passage, but don't count on bending it all the way to an E—it won't happen. The partial bends are marked with a (~) symbol. In hole 6 blow there's a partial bend (~) that doesn't quite reach a true G♭ note before you hit a B♭ overblow note. This is also the case with the hole 7 blow C note. You can bend the C note down into the B range (~) but not all the way to a "true" B note. There is a B draw note in the same hole.

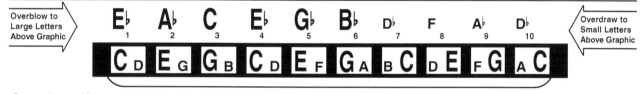

Overbending The letters above the holes in the harmonica represent the notes you can overbend to. You overblow in holes 1 through 6 and overdraw in holes 7 through 10. Overbending is an advanced technique and requires fine-tuned breath control, practice and persistence to achieve. (See page 11.)

Hollow Letters The hollow letters in the holes represent notes you don't play in an exercise. Play only the notes represented by **black** letters. In the example above, the **black** letters are C-E-G, C-D-E-F-G-A-B-C. When you play the **black** letters from left to right, one note at a time, you'll blow a C arpeggio in the low octave and then in the middle octave, blow and draw a C major scale. Remember not to play the hollow letters.

Letters Outside The Harmonica Graphic represent bend and overbend notes. The bend and overbend notes that are not being played in an example will *not* appear as hollow letters outside the graphic. They don't appear at all. Only the note that you "bend to" will appear over or under the hole as a **black** letter. The example above shows a two octave C major scale. **Note:** Because they are not part of the C major scale, the G♭ bend in hole 2 and the A♭ and B♭ bends in hole 3 do not appear under the graphic. Only the F and A bends are shown. All the other bend and overbend notes not used in an example do not appear.

The Staff and Notes

Hole Numbers 1   2   3   4   5   6   7   8   9   10

The Staff above the harmonica graphic is divided into ten measures—one measure per hole. The following symbol (8va----------------) appears above notes that are played an octave higher than written.

Quarter Notes, Eighth Notes and Slurs Quarter notes represent the reed names. A single note that is bent or overbent appears as an 1/8 note. Two or more notes sounded from a common reed are connected with a slur. An overbend note that occurs with the primary reed note will also be connected with a slur when they are played in the same hole. Disregard the time value usually attributed to notes. Here notes are used to show the pitch of a reed or a note derived from a bend or overbend. Play each note as long as it takes to learn the skill shown in the example. In this book, the focus is on pitch, not rhythm.

A 1/4 note indicates the name of the reed you play in the hole shown below it. A reed note.

An 1/8 note indicates a note that is bent or overbent, in the hole directly below.

A beam If there is more than one bend note in a single hole, they will be connected with a beam.

A slur connecting two notes shows notes sounded from a common reed or an overbend and the primary reed note.

Putting the Graphic and Staff Together

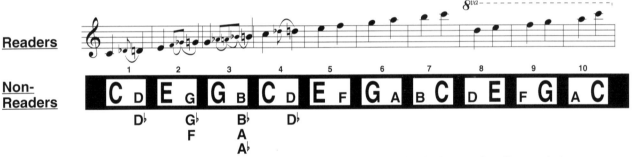

Readers

Non-Readers

Reading Musicians Match the notes on the staff to the corresponding holes in the harmonica diagram below.
Non-reading Musicians Blow and draw the appropriate **black** letters and learn how the corresponding written music looks on the staff above.

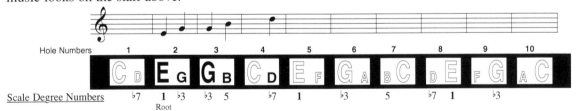

Hole Numbers 1   2   3   4   5   6   7   8   9   10

Scale Degree Numbers ♭7 **1** ♭3   ♭3   5   ♭7 **1**   ♭3   5   ♭7 **1** ♭3
Root

Numbers Below the Graphic The numbers directly under the harmonica graphic represent scale degrees. The root will have a bold (**1**) under it wherever it occurs. There will be a sharp symbol (#) or a flat symbol (♭) next to the number if the note is enharmonic. (See page 13.) The example above shows an Em7 arpeggio in holes 2, 3 and 4. The notes appear on the staff above the graphic. The graphic shows the letter names of those notes. The number under a **black** letter identifies the degree of the arpeggio, or scale, for the note directly above. In any example, the scale degree numbers under the hollow letters identify additional notes in the arpeggio that you can use to create alternative inversions or voicings.
Holes 2 and 3 both have the same G note in them—a draw G in hole 2 and a blow G in hole 3. Sometimes they will both be highlighted as **black** letters in an example, but you need only play one of them. Without overbending, this is the sole opportunity to catch your breath by either drawing or blowing the same note.

Playing Single Notes

Pucker, Pursed Lip or Straw Method

This is probably the way you played the first single note on your original harp. Some call it the straw method, because you shape your lips the same way you do when you use a straw to sip a drink. Others call it lipping, or the pursed lip method, pursed meaning to pucker. Another way to describe this technique is that the shape of your mouth is similar to when you whistle. The object is to pucker your lips so you only play one note at a time. Make sure there is an airtight seal between your mouth and the harmonica. This conserves air and gives you more control when bending notes. It also leaves your tongue free to finesse the direction and pressure of the air flow.

Whistle

D note—drawn.

Tongue Blocking

This is a another popular method used by many players. First, put your mouth over four holes as if you are going to play four notes at the same time. Then, with your tongue, block three holes and blow or draw a single note. You can also cover three holes with your mouth and block two of the holes with your tongue. Use the method that is more comfortable.

Tongue Left—Hole Right Method Keep your tongue to the left, creating the air passage on the right. This method is more commonly used than the tongue right method.

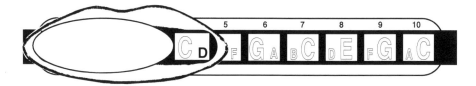

Tongue Right—Hole Left Method Keep your tongue to the right, creating the air passage to the left.

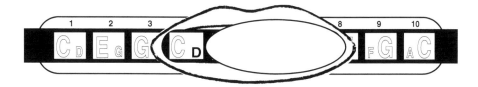

Curled Tongue Method

This method is reserved for a player who is genetically predisposed with the ability to curl his tongue into a "U" shape. This is also called "U blocking" or "tube tonguing" and allows more control when bending and overbending. It facilitates maximum control of the air flow, right up to the harmonica's air channel.

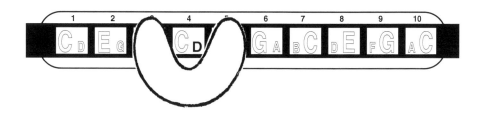

Understanding Intervals

Western music is derived from a scale that is made up of 12 equally-spaced notes called the "chromatic scale." The distance between each of those 12 notes is a "half step." Two half steps are called a "whole step." Three half steps are called "a step and a half," and so on. The musical distance between any two notes is called an "interval." There are terms that describe any given pair of notes or intervals. These are the most common.

- **1/2 step = minor second** (♭2)
- **Whole step = Major second** (2)
- **One & 1/2 steps = minor third** (♭3)
- **Two steps = Major third** (3)
- **Two & 1/2 steps = Perfect Fourth** (4)
- **Three steps = diminished fifth** (♭5) **tritone or** ᵃᵘᵍ4 (#4)
- **Three & 1/2 steps = Perfect Fifth** (5)
- **Four steps = minor sixth** (♭6) **or** ᵃᵘᵍ5 (#5)
- **Four & 1/2 steps = Major sixth** (6) **or** ᵈⁱᵐ7 (♭♭7)
- **Five steps = minor seventh** (♭7)
- **Five & 1/2 steps = Major seventh** (ᴹᵃʲ7) (△7)
- **Six steps = Octave**

Intervals: 10-hole C Major Diatonic Harp—Richter System

The difference between learning music on a harmonica and a guitar or a keyboard is that guitars and keyboards are designed using all 1/2 steps. The diatonic harmonica is not.

Harmonicas based on the Richter arrangement are all made up of the same sequence of intervals derived from a fixed combination of minor 2nds, major 2nds, minor 3rds, major 3rds and perfect 4ths. On the C harp, in holes 2 and 3, the same G note appears in both—hole 2 draw and hole 3 blow.

Remember: To play all 20 ascending notes continuously, blow then draw in holes 1 through 6, then change to draw then blow in holes 7 through 10. The interval spacing will be the same on every 10-hole major diatonic harmonica regardless of the key. Only the key and notes will be transposed.

Blow intervals

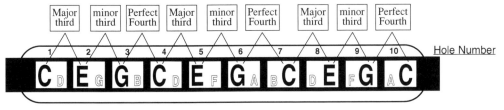

- The blow reeds are connected to the reed plate, closest to the mouthpiece. They vibrate as the air travels through the air channel, past the reed and out the back side of the harmonica.

Consecutive intervals blow and draw

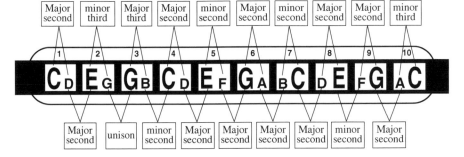

Draw intervals

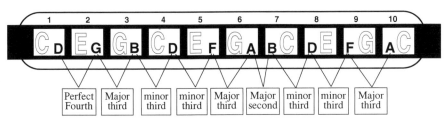

- The draw reeds are connected to the reed plate, farthest from the mouthpiece. They vibrate as the air travels into the back side of the harmonica, past the reed, through the air channel in the comb, and into your mouth.

THE RANGE OF THE C 10-HOLE DIATONIC HARMONICA

Beginning

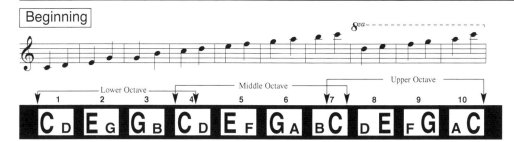

Reed Notes

- These are the names of the reeds manufacturers put into the key of C diatonic harmonica.

Intermediate

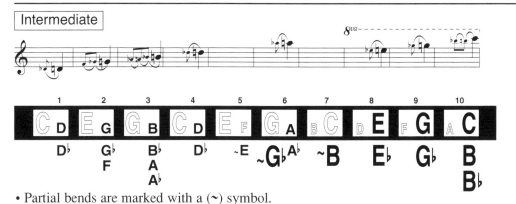

- Partial bends are marked with a (∼) symbol.

Bending

- Draw to bend in holes 1–6.
- Blow to bend in holes 6–10.
- Partial bends only in 5 draw, 6 blow and 7 blow.

Advanced

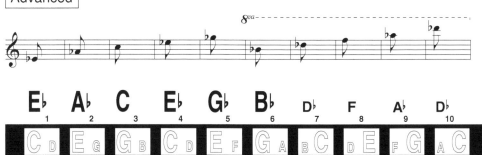

Overbending

- Overblow in holes 1–6.
- Overdraw in holes 7–10.
- By overbending you can play all of the notes not found through bending or playing reed notes.

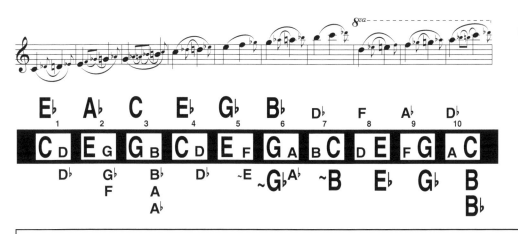

C Harp All Notes

- All available notes including bending, overblowing and overdrawing.
- Two overbend notes have identical reed notes in the hole to the right—the C in hole 3 and the F in hole 8.

Playing the C Diatonic Harp Chromatically: When you play the notes manufactured into this 10-hole major diatonic harmonica combined with bending, overblowing and overdrawing, you can play over three full chromatic octaves—middle C to C# (D♭). (See page 38.)

Bending Notes

Bending a note is achieved by changing the characteristics (the size and shape) of the air chamber formed by your tongue and mouth, in addition to modifying the air pressure and direction of its flow through the hole and past the reeds.

When you bend a note, the shape of your mouth should be similar to the shape of your mouth when you whistle descending notes. Try this: while breathing in, whistle a high note and then slowly lower its pitch. Notice the movement and position of your tongue. Practice the inhale whistle by imitating the sound of a WWII bomb dropping. Now try a bend. While drawing in hole 4, close off the air passage to your nose and do the same thing with your tongue that you do when

you whistle from a high note to a low note. You should hear it bend. Modify your tongue movement until you get a good, solid bend note. Therein lies the heart of the blues harp sound.

For lower note bends, lower your jaw while simultaneously moving your tongue back in your mouth in a way that channels and constricts the passage of air. This causes the primary reed to slow, which lowers its pitch. That, in turn, initiates sympathetic vibration on the other (non-primary) reed in the hole. As more of the vibration transfers from the primary to the non-primary reed, it facilitates even further vibration of the non-primary reed and a lower pitch or bend note. When you play a draw bend, the non-primary blow reed may ultimately create the lower note. (See "How The Air Flows" on page 47.) This technique allows you to produce, for example, a D♭ note from the D draw reed in hole 1 or an A♭, A, or B♭ note from the B draw reed in hole 3, etc. It can also provide the means needed to produce vibrato and tremolo effects so essential to producing a sweeter sounding note.

Bending the higher blow notes in holes 8, 9 and 10 requires modifying your technique. Your tongue should be more forward in your mouth, creating a smaller air chamber. You'll need to exert less air pressure, too. The higher the blow bend note, the smaller the air chamber needs to be. The lower the blow bend note, the larger the air chamber needs to be.

On the higher blow bends, it's the draw reed that ultimately creates the lower pitched bend note.

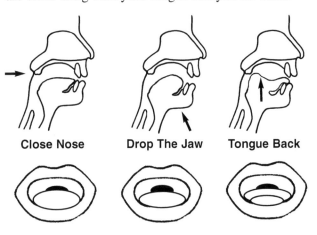

Close Nose   **Drop The Jaw**   **Tongue Back**

The Bend Intervals
Draw Bends
Hole 1: You can bend this D note down a little more than 1/2 step, so you might want to practice getting it to go exactly to a D♭ (C#).

Hole 2: This G note bends down 1/2 step to G♭ (F#) and also a whole step to F. Bending only 1/2 step requires a little more control.

Hole 3: Bend this B note down 1/2 step to B♭ (A#), a whole step to A or 1-1/2 steps to A♭ (G#). Bending exactly to the notes in between takes a little practice, but it's a very useful and rewarding skill.

Hole 4: This D note bends down 1/2 step to D♭ (C#).

Hole 5: This F note almost bends down 1/2 step to E, but not quite. The ~E denotes the partial bend.

Hole 6: This A note bends down 1/2 step to A♭ (G#).

Blow Bends
Hole 6: Partial bend. G almost bends to G♭ (F#). ~G♭.

Hole 7: Partial bend. The C almost bends 1/2 step down to a B but not quite. This ~B symbol is used.

Hole 8: This E note bends down 1/2 step to E♭ (D#).

Hole 9: This G note bends down 1/2 step to G♭ (F#).

Hole 10: This C note bends down a half step to B or a whole step to B♭ (A#). You'll probably hit the whole step first and have to practice getting the 1/2 step bend. It takes a little more control.

Hitting a Note Pre-bent
Scales and arpeggios in some positions require you to play a note or notes pre-bent. Here's an exercise to try in holes 1 and 2: Draw the G note in hole 2 and then bend it down to the G♭. Keeping your tongue in that same position, quickly move to hole 1. You should now be drawing a D (non-bent) note with your tongue still in the position for the hole 2 G♭ bend. Quickly move back to hole 2 and you will hit the pre-bent G♭ note. Relax your tongue and return to the unbent G note. Once you know the position your tongue needs to be in and the air pressure required for a particular bend, you can return to that pre-bent note anytime.

Harps in Higher Keys
D♭, D, E♭, E, F, F# and the high-tuned G, A♭ and A harps. Bending notes on harps in higher keys requires your tongue to be farther forward with a tighter constriction of the air chamber in your mouth. It takes less air pressure to produce the bend.

Harps in Lower Keys
B, B♭, A, A♭, G and the low-tuned F#, F, E, E♭ and D harps. Bending notes on harps in lower keys requires a larger air chamber because the lower notes have a longer wave length. You'll need to create a longer, more open air chamber, including your throat. Bending notes on harps in lower keys requires a little more breath.

Overbending Notes

This is an advanced technique which requires a lot of time to master. To reach a specific overbend note you'll have to control your breath and align the shape of the inside of your mouth to coincide with the frequency of the desired note. This will create the characteristic in the air flow needed to start the movement of the non-primary opening reed. It's tricky business, but can be predictably achieved through persistence and practice. There is a lot of trial and error involved in learning this advanced technique. To help facilitate the overbend, many players adjust the clearance of the reeds closer to the reed plate. (Refer to page 47.)

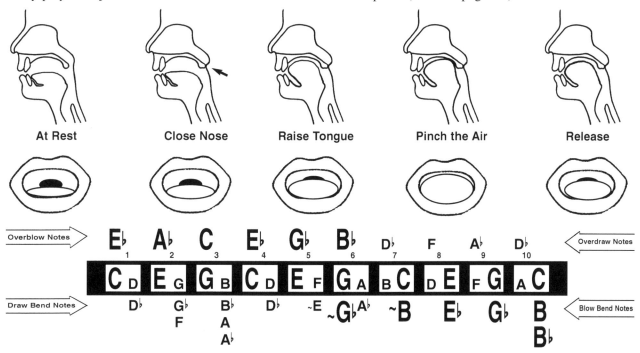

Overbending is a general term used to describe overblowing and overdrawing. None of the chords, modes or arpeggios in this book require overbending —only the advanced scales on pages 38–41. It's easier to overbend on harps in lower keys than higher keys.

Overblowing Overblowing occurs when you blow into a hole and create a pitch 1/2 step higher than the draw reed. To overblow in holes 1 through 6, tighten your upper lip and quickly release a constricted flow of air from deep within your lungs. This causes the draw reed to vibrate at a slightly faster rate than it was designed to. Make sure your tongue is towards the top of your mouth and quickly release the air pressure. The blow reed is the closing reed and its interaction with the air flow causes the draw reed to produce the overblow note.

Overblowing hole 6 uses a similar technique to the one used when doing the blow bend in holes 8 through 10. You can bend the pitch of overblow notes, too.

Overdrawing When you draw air through a hole and create a pitch 1/2 step higher than the blow reed note, it is called overdrawing. This is achieved by drawing air through a hole (7, 8, 9 or 10), causing the vibration of the higher-pitched blow reed, which in turn creates the overdraw note. It is the opposite of overblowing.

The Overbend Intervals
Overblows
Hole 1: You can overblow the D draw reed up 1/2 step to an E♭ (D#). It requires very little air pressure.
Hole 2: You can overblow the G draw reed up 1/2 step to A♭ (G#). The A♭ bend in hole 3 is easier to play.
Hole 3: Overblow the B draw reed up 1/2 step to a C note. It's a lot easier to play that same C note by blowing in hole 4.
Hole 4: You can overblow the D draw reed up 1/2 step to an E♭ (D#) note.
Hole 5: You can overblow the F draw reed up 1/2 step to a G♭ (F#).
Hole 6: You can overblow the A draw reed up 1/2 step to B♭ (A#). You can almost reach a G♭ (~G♭) blow bend, just before you hit the B♭ (A#) overblow.

Overdraws
Hole 7: You can overdraw the C blow reed up 1/2 step to a D♭ (C#) note.
Hole 8: You can overdraw the E blow reed up 1/2 step to an F. The draw F in hole 9 is easier to play.
Hole 9: You can overdraw the G blow reed up 1/2 step to an A♭ (G#) note.
Hole 10: You can overdraw the C blow reed up 1/2 step to a D♭ (C#) note.

C Harp Relative to Other Instruments

The illustrations below will help you visualize where notes on a C harp appear on other instruments. The examples show notes that represent reeds, without bending or overbending.

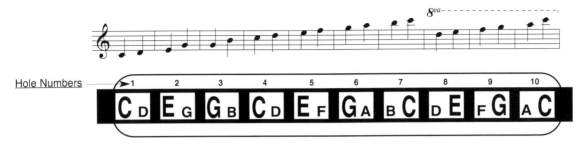

C Diatonic Harmonica and the Keyboard

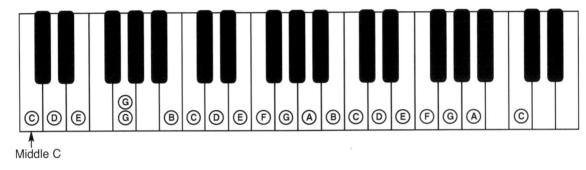

Middle C

C Diatonic Harmonica and the Guitar

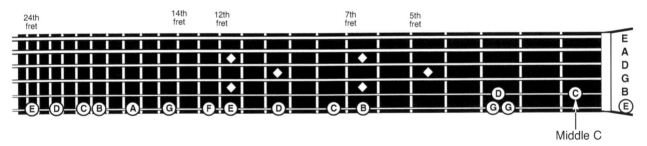

Middle C

The typical acoustic guitar fingerboard meets the body at the 14th fret. The length of an electric guitar fretboard varies, depending on the model. A 24-fret fingerboard is shown here. The standard guitar doesn't have enough frets to accommodate the highest notes on a C harmonica. This chart can be helpful in choosing which harmonica to use when simulating bending strings on the guitar. Match the bend notes from a guitar string to the bending chart on page 9 to see if a C harp has the right available bends. If not, look through the other books in this series. Find which harp has the correct bends, so you'll know which is the right one for the job.

C Diatonic Harmonica and the Mandolin

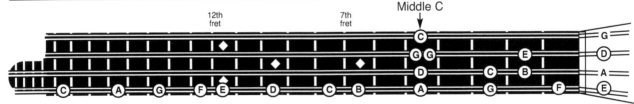

The mandolin and violin are tuned the same. This chart will also work for the violin. Vibrato, legato or glissando in violin music can also be achieved by bending notes on the harmonica.

Understanding the C Major Diatonic Scale ...

The chromatic scale is made up of 12 equally-spaced tones. Seven of them are named after the first seven letters in the English alphabet. They are A, B, C, D, E, F and G. The other five notes were given names based on whether they are lower or higher than the note they are next to. If it's higher, it is called sharp ($\#$). If it is lower, it's called flat ($\flat$). So the note that's 1/2 step higher than A is called A$\#$. The note that's 1/2 step lower than A is called A$\flat$, and so on. There is no sharp note or flat note between the B and C notes or the E and F notes. The term used to describe a note with two names is "enharmonic." For example, the enharmonic note between the A and B notes can either be called A$\#$ or B$\flat$, depending on whether you are referring to the note as being above A or below B. Whether a note is called sharp or flat will also be determined by the key signature.

The 12-tone Western Scale is more commonly called the "chromatic scale."

| C | C$\#$ / D$\flat$ | D | D$\#$ / E$\flat$ | E | F | F$\#$ / G$\flat$ | G | G$\#$ / A$\flat$ | A | A$\#$ / B$\flat$ | B | C |

The Major Diatonic Scale A diatonic scale is a seven-note scale with each of the notes in the musical alphabet included (C, D, E, F, G, A and B.) The system of numbers used to identify scale degrees and chord construction is based on the major diatonic scale. The scale degrees are referred to as the 1st, 2nd, 3rd, 4th, 5th, 6th and 7th degree. One number is assigned to each letter. Scale degree numbers that are not part of the major scale are identified with a ($\#$) or ($\flat$) symbol. The 1st degree is the root. Expressed as intervals the major scale formula is: whole step, whole step, half step, whole step, whole step, whole step, half step.

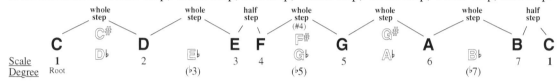

	whole step		whole step		half step		whole step (#4)		whole step		whole step		half step	
C	C$\#$ / D$\flat$	D	E$\flat$	E	F	F$\#$ / G$\flat$		G	G$\#$ / A$\flat$	A	B$\flat$	B	C

Scale Degree: 1 (Root), 2, ($\flat$3) 3, 4, ($\flat$5) 5, 6, ($\flat$7) 7, 1

Pentatonic Scales have five notes and are commonly used in playing the blues. The major pentatonic scale includes the root (**1**), 2, 3, 5 and 6 degrees of the major scale. C major pentatonic scale = C-D-E-G-A. The minor pentatonic scale includes the root (**1**), $\flat$3, 4, 5 and $\flat$7 degrees of the major scale. Cm pentatonic scale = C-E$\flat$-F-G-B$\flat$.

Its Seven Modes and 12 Positions.

C Major Scale Mode Chart The intervals between the notes in the modes below are designated in parentheses with a "W" for a whole step and "1/2" for a half step. The C major scale = C Ionian mode.

Do Re Mi Fa Sol La Ti Do Re Mi Fa Sol La Ti Do
C D E F G A B C D E F G A B C
W W 1/2 W W W 1/2 W W 1/2 W W W 1/2

C D E F G A B C	**C Ionian mode** or **C Major scale** – (w, w, 1/2, w, w, w, 1/2)
D E F G A B C D	**D Dorian mode** – (w, 1/2, w, w, w, 1/2, w)
E F G A B C D E	**E Phrygian mode** – (1/2, w, w, w, 1/2, w, w)
F G A B C D E F	**F Lydian mode** – (w, w, w, 1/2, w, w, 1/2)
G A B C D E F G	**G Mixolydian mode** – (w, w, 1/2, w, w, 1/2, w)
A B C D E F G A	**A Aeolian mode** – (w, 1/2, w, w, 1/2, w, w)
B C D E F G A B	**B Locrian mode** – (1/2, w, w, 1/2 w, w, w)

Positions Many harmonica players refer to modes as positions.

1st position: C Ionian mode.
2nd position: G Mixolydian mode.
3rd position: D Dorian mode.
4th position: A Aeolian mode.
5th position: E Phrygian mode.
6th position: B Locrian mode.
12th position: F Lydian mode.

Positions six through 11 are not commonly used.

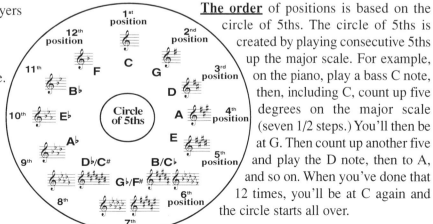

The order of positions is based on the circle of 5ths. The circle of 5ths is created by playing consecutive 5ths up the major scale. For example, on the piano, play a bass C note, then, including C, count up five degrees on the major scale (seven 1/2 steps.) You'll then be at G. Then count up another five and play the D note, then to A, and so on. When you've done that 12 times, you'll be at C again and the circle starts all over.

C Major Scale — Ionian Mode

The C Ionian mode begins on the 1st degree of the C major scale, or "do."

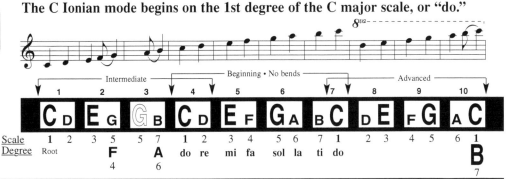

- **Straight Harp**
C Ionian Mode:
C D E F G A B C
1 2 3 4 5 6 7 1
- There are draw bends in hole 2 (F), hole 3 (A) and a blow bend in hole 10 (B).

FIRST POSITION • Variations on Ionian for playing C Blues

C Mixolydian

- The following scales may require bending to the ♭3, ♭5 or ♭7 "blue notes."

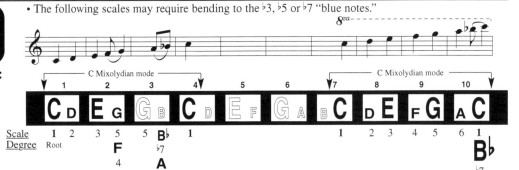

C Mixolydian Mode:
C D E F G A B♭ C
1 2 3 4 5 6 ♭7 1
- C Mixolydian is simply C Ionian with a ♭7.
- Draw the A and B♭ notes in hole 3 bent.

C Dorian Mode

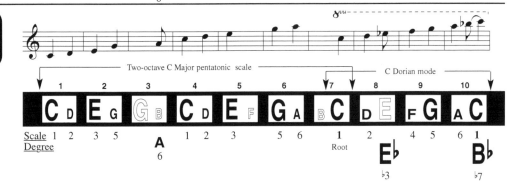

C Dorian Mode:
C D E♭ F G A B♭ C
1 2 ♭3 4 5 6 ♭7 1
- Flat the 3rd (E to E♭) of C Mixolydian.

C Major Pentatonic:
- Play: C D E G A C
1 2 3 5 6 1

C Blues Scale

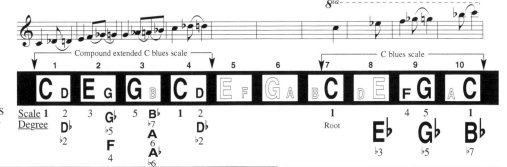

C Blues Scale:
C E♭ F G♭ G B♭ C
1 ♭3 4 ♭5 5 ♭7 1
- On the low end, blues riffs can be played by combining segments of different C scales.

Playing C Blues

- Use your C harp to play blues in the key of C.
- Resolve the V chord (G) on any G note.

Blow bend the ♭3 E♭, ♭5 G♭ and ♭7 B♭ in the high octave or bend between the C and ~B in hole 7. Blow bend between E and E♭ in hole 8. During the IV chord (F), draw bend between the A and A♭ notes in hole 6. By combining parts of the chromatic, pentatonic and blues scales on the lower end of the harp, many blues riffs can be played in the key of C. (See "More Blues Scales" on page 21.)

Key of C
12-bar Blues Chord Progression:

C—	C—	C—	C—
1 2 3 4 •	1 2 3 4 •	1 2 3 4 •	1 2 3 4
F—	F—	C—	C—
1 2 3 4 •	1 2 3 4 •	1 2 3 4 •	1 2 3 4
G—	F—	C—	G—
1 2 3 4 •	1 2 3 4 •	1 2 3 4 •	1 2 3 4

(Each chord is played four beats.)

The G Mixolydian mode begins on the 5th degree of the C major scale, or "sol."

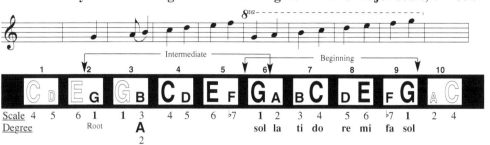

G7 Scale Mixolydian

- **Cross Harp**
- **G Mixolydian Mode:**
G A B C D E F G
1 2 3 4 5 6 ♭7 1
- 2nd position begins in hole 2 draw.
- Major scale with ♭7.

• In addition to blues and rock, many Appalachian and British Isles fiddle tunes are written in Mixolydian.

SECOND POSITION • Variations on Mixolydian for Playing G Blues

• The following scales may require bending to the ♭3, ♭5 or ♭7 blue notes.

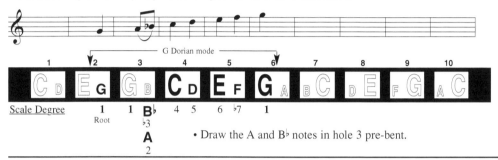

G Dorian Mode

G Dorian Mode:
G A B♭ C D E F G
1 2 ♭3 4 5 6 ♭7 1
- When you flat the third (B to B♭) of G Mixolydian, you get the G Dorian mode.

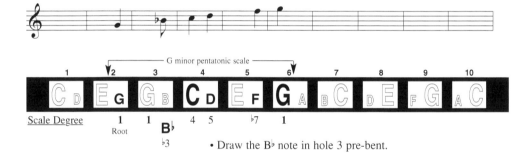

Gm Pentatonic Scale

G Minor Pentatonic:
G B♭ C D F G
1 ♭3 4 5 ♭7 1
- Omit the 2nd and 6th degrees of the G Dorian mode, and you get the G minor pentatonic scale.

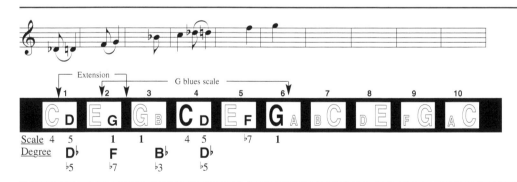

G Blues Scale

G Blues Scale:
G B♭ C D♭ D F G
1 ♭3 4 ♭5 5 ♭7 1
- When you add the ♭5 D♭ to the Gm pentatonic scale, you get the G blues scale.

Key of G
12-bar Blues Chord Progression:

G— G— G— G—
1 2 3 4 • 1 2 3 4 • 1 2 3 4 • 1 2 3 4
C— C— G— G—
1 2 3 4 • 1 2 3 4 • 1 2 3 4 • 1 2 3 4
D— C— G— D—
1 2 3 4 • 1 2 3 4 • 1 2 3 4 • 1 2 3 4

(Each chord is played four beats.)

Second position starts with a draw G note in hole 2. With the ♭5 D♭ bend in holes 1 and 4, the ♭3 B♭ in hole 3 and the ♭7 F bend in hole 2, the first four holes play an important part in the second position blues harp style. Extend the G scale beyond hole 6 to find additional notes to play. Blow bend between the G and G♭ in hole 9. (See "More Blues Scales" on page 21.)

Playing G Blues

- Use your C harp to play blues in the key of G.
- Resolve the V chord (D) on any D note.

THIRD POSITION • D Dorian Mode

Dm7 Scale
Dorian Mode

D Dorian Mode:
D E F G A B C D
1 2 ♭3 4 5 6 ♭7 1
- Double-crossed, Slant Harp or Draw Harp.
- 3rd position begins in the 4th hole draw.

The D Dorian mode begins on the 2nd degree of the C major scale, or "re."

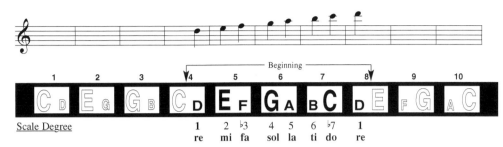

- This mode is commonly used to play rock, blues, country and folk tunes in minor keys.

Dm7 Scale
Dorian Mode
with bends

- 3rd position with bends begins in the 1st hole draw.
- Practice hitting the hole 3, A draw bent.
- Dorian: ♭3 and ♭7.

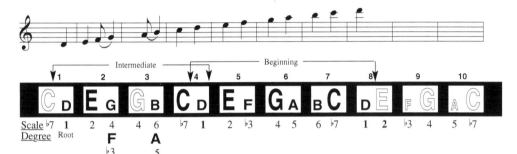

THIRD POSITION • Variations on Dorian for Playing D Blues

Dm Pentatonic Scale

D Minor Pentatonic:
- Play D F G A C D
  1 ♭3 4 5 ♭7 1
- Minor pentatonic scales are five-note scales without any half steps.

- The following scales may require bending to the ♭3 or ♭5 blue notes.

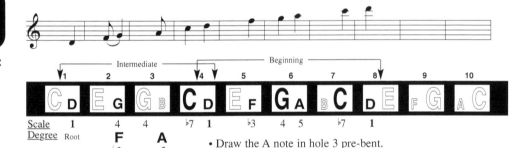

- Draw the A note in hole 3 pre-bent.

D Blues Scale

D Blues Scale:
D F G A♭ A C D
1 ♭3 4 ♭5 5 ♭7 1
- Add a ♭5 A♭ to the Dm pentatonic scale to get a D blues scale.

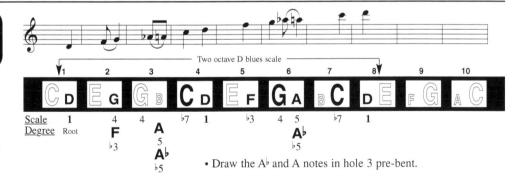

- Draw the A♭ and A notes in hole 3 pre-bent.

Playing D Blues

- Use your C harp to play blues in the key of D or Dm.
- Resolve the V chord (A) on any A note.

A full two-octave D blues scale can be played in holes 1 through 8. The ♭3 F in hole 2 is a whole step draw bend. There are Dm chords and dyads in the middle and upper octaves. Try draw bending between the D and D♭ in holes 1 and 4. In the first four holes you can draw all of the notes in the D blues scale except C. The draw IV chord (G) is found in holes 1–4. (See "More Blues Scales" on page 21.)

Key of D
12-bar Blues Chord Progression:

D—	D—	D—	D—
1 2 3 4 •	1 2 3 4 •	1 2 3 4 •	1 2 3 4

G—	G—	D—	D—
1 2 3 4 •	1 2 3 4 •	1 2 3 4 •	1 2 3 4

A—	G—	D—	A—
1 2 3 4 •	1 2 3 4 •	1 2 3 4 •	1 2 3 4

(Each chord is played four beats.)

The A Aeolian mode begins on the 6th degree of the C major scale, or "la."

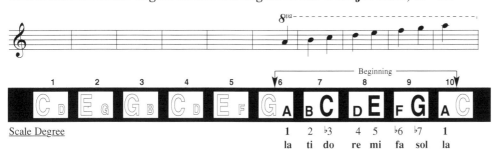

Scale Degree — 1 2 ♭3 4 5 ♭6 ♭7 1 / la ti do re mi fa sol la

A Natural Minor Scale

A Aeolian Mode:
A B C D E F G A
1 2 ♭3 4 5 ♭6 ♭7 1
- The easiest way to play the A natural minor scale begins in hole 6 draw.
- Aeolian: ♭3, ♭6 & ♭7.

- Used in minor key tunes and Eastern European, Middle Eastern, Mediterranean and Gypsy music.

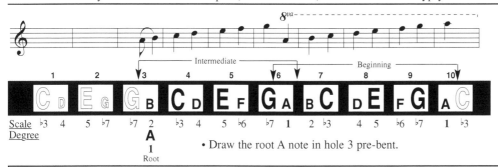

Scale Degree — ♭3 4 5 ♭7 ♭7 2 ♭3 4 5 ♭6 ♭7 1 2 ♭3 4 5 ♭6 ♭7 1 ♭3

A 1 Root

- Draw the root A note in hole 3 pre-bent.

A Natural Minor Scale with a bend

- Two octave scale begins with a draw bend in the 3rd hole.
- Practice hitting the root A pre-bent without sliding into it.

FOURTH POSITION • Variations on Aeolian for Playing A Blues

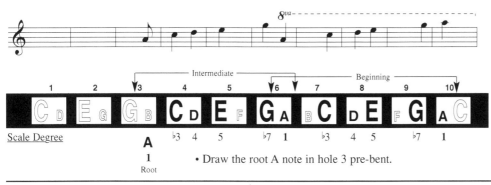

Scale Degree — A 1 Root ♭3 4 5 ♭7 1 ♭3 4 5 ♭7 1

- Draw the root A note in hole 3 pre-bent.

Am Pentatonic Scale

A Minor Pentatonic:
- Play A C D E G A
  1 ♭3 4 5 ♭7 1
- Omit the 2nd and 6th degrees of an A natural minor scale and you get the Am pentatonic scale.

- The following blues scale requires bending to the ♭5 blue note.

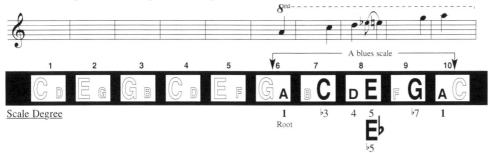

Scale Degree — 1 Root ♭3 4 5 ♭7 1 / E♭ ♭5

A Blues Scale

A Blues Scale:
A C D E♭ E G A
1 ♭3 4 ♭5 5 ♭7 1
- Add a ♭5 E♭ to the Am pentatonic scale to get an A blues scale.

**Key of Am
12-bar Blues Chord Progression:**
Am— Dm— Am— Am—
1 2 3 4 • 1 2 3 4 • 1 2 3 4 • 1 2 3 4
Dm — Dm — Am— Am—
1 2 3 4 • 1 2 3 4 • 1 2 3 4 • 1 2 3 4
Em — Dm — Am Dm Am E
1 2 3 4 • 1 2 3 4 • 1 2 3 4 1 2 3 4
(Each chord is played four beats.)

Draw bend between the A and the A♭ in hole 6. Blow bend between C and ~B in hole 7 and the G and G♭ in hole 9. You can extend the Am pentatonic scale down into the first three holes by using the G, E, D and C notes. Draw bend between the G and F notes in hole 2. Am is the relative minor of C, so try playing bits of the C scales on page 21 when playing blues in the key of either A or Am.

Playing Am Blues

- Use your C harp to play blues in the key of Am or A.
- Resolve the V chord (E) on any E note.

E Phrygian (minor)

The E Phrygian mode begins on the 3rd degree of the C major scale, or "mi."

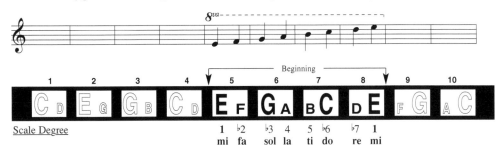

E Phrygian Mode:
E F G A B C D E
1 ♭2 ♭3 4 5 ♭6 ♭7 1
• 5th position begins on the 5th hole blow.
• Phrygian: ♭2, ♭3, ♭6 and ♭7.

E Phrygian (minor) with bends

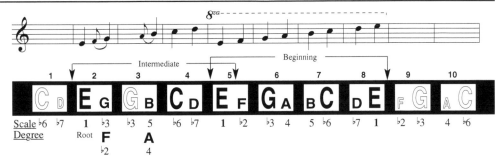

• 5th position two octave run begins on the 2nd hole blow.
• Two bends. The F in hole 2 and the A in hole 3.

• You'll find this mode is used frequently in Middle Eastern music.

FIFTH POSITION • Variations on Phrygian for Playing E Blues

Em Pentatonic Scale

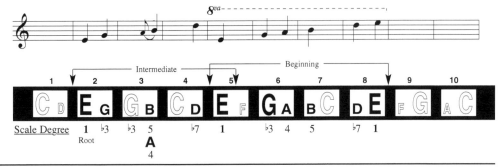

E Minor Pentatonic:
• Play E G A B D E
1 ♭3 4 5 ♭7 1
• Em pentatonic scale is a five-tone scale used in playing blues in the key of E.

E Blues Scale

• The following blues scale requires bending to the ♭5 blue note.

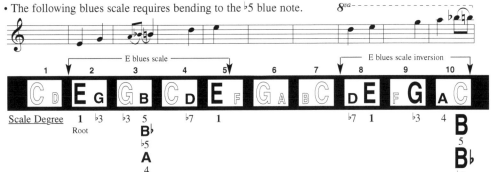

E Blues Scale:
E G A B♭ B D E
1 ♭3 4 ♭5 5 ♭7 1
• Add the ♭5 B♭ note to the Em pentatonic scale and you get an E blues scale.

Playing E Blues

• Use your C harp to play blues in the key of E or Em.
• Resolve the V chord (B) on any B note.

The easiest E blues riffs are on the lower end, with plenty of bending in the third hole. You'll find ♭3 G notes to play by drawing in hole 2 and blowing in holes 3, 6 and 9. Use the draw A and B in holes 6 and 7. During the IV and V chords draw bend between the A and A♭ in hole 6. Blow bend between the E and E♭ in the high octave. E is a key that guitarists seem to favor when playing blues. (See "More Blues Scales" on page 21.)

**Key of E
12-bar Blues Chord Progression:**

E—	E—	E—	E—
1 2 3 4 •	1 2 3 4 •	1 2 3 4 •	1 2 3 4
A—	A—	E—	E—
1 2 3 4 •	1 2 3 4 •	1 2 3 4 •	1 2 3 4
B—	A—	E—	B—
1 2 3 4 •	1 2 3 4 •	1 2 3 4 •	1 2 3 4

(Each chord is played four beats.)

SIXTH POSITION • B Locrian Mode

The B Locrian mode begins on the 7th degree of the C major scale, or "ti."

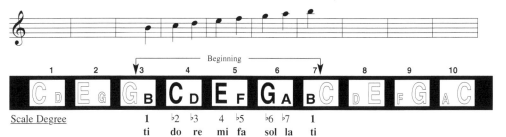

B Locrian (minor)

B Locrian Mode:
B C D E F G A B
1 ♭2 ♭3 4 ♭5 ♭6 ♭7 1

• 6th position begins on the 3rd hole draw.

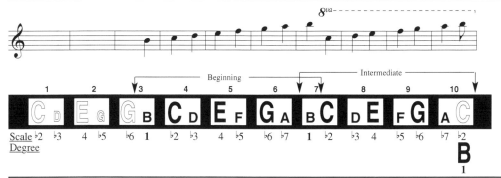

B Locrian (minor) with a bend

• Locrian Mode: ♭2, ♭3, ♭5, ♭6 and ♭7.
• In hole 10 blow the B note pre-bent.
• 6th position with a bend begins on the 3rd hole draw.

SIXTH POSITION • Variations on Locrian for Playing B Blues

• The following scales may require bending to the ♭5 or ♭7 blue notes.

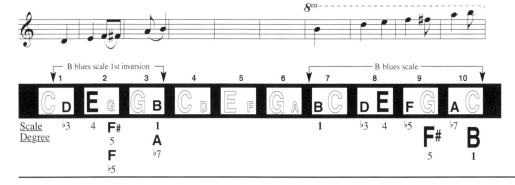

B Blues Scale

B Blues Scale:
B D E F F# A B
1 ♭3 4 ♭5 5 ♭7 1

• Omit the ♭2 and ♭6 from B Locrian then add the perfect fifth (F#). Draw the F and F# in hole 2 bent.

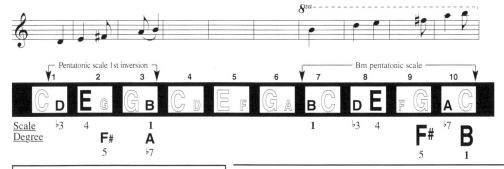

Bm Pentatonic Scale

Bm Pentatonic Scale:
B D E F# A B
1 ♭3 4 5 ♭7 1

• Omit the ♭5 F from the B blues scale to get the Bm pentatonic scale.

**Key of B
12-bar Blues Chord Progression:**

B— B— B— B—
1 2 3 4 • 1 2 3 4 • 1 2 3 4 • 1 2 3 4

E— E— B— B—
1 2 3 4 • 1 2 3 4 • 1 2 3 4 • 1 2 3 4

F#— E— B— F#—
1 2 3 4 • 1 2 3 4 • 1 2 3 4 • 1 2 3 4

(Each chord is played four beats.)

Bend your way through the B blues scale (1st inversion) in the lower octave with almost all draw notes. In holes 1 and 4 try bending the D. In hole 6, bend between the A and A♭. Play the root B often. What sets sixth position apart from the others is that the resolution note of the V chord is a bent F#. Draw the perfect 5th (F#) in hole 2 pre-bent. Learn it and rely on it. Play octave trills on the I (B) and IV (E) chords.

Playing B Blues

• Use your C harp when playing blues in B or Bm.
• Resolve the V chord (F#) on any F# note.

19

F Lydian (Major)

F Lydian Mode:
F G A B C D E F
1 2 3 #4 5 6 7 1

- 12th position begins in the 5th hole draw.
- Lydian: #4. Raise the 4th degree (B♭ to B) of the major scale.

The F Lydian mode begins on the 4th degree of the C major scale, or "fa."

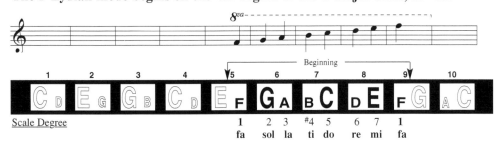

First Flat Position: When moving around the circle of fifths in the flat (♭) direction (counterclockwise) beginning at the root C note, F is the first key you come to. (See page 13.)

F Lydian (Major) with bends

- 12th position two octave run begins in the 2nd hole with the draw F pre-bent.
- When playing blues think of the #4 as a ♭5.

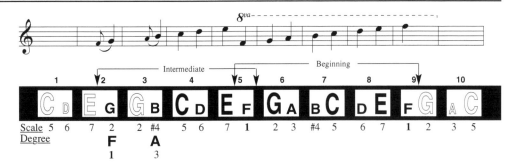

TWELFTH POSITION • Variations on Lydian for Playing F Blues

F Major Pentatonic Scale

F Major Pentatonic Scale:
F G A C D F
1 2 3 5 6 1

- Beginners start in hole 5 draw.

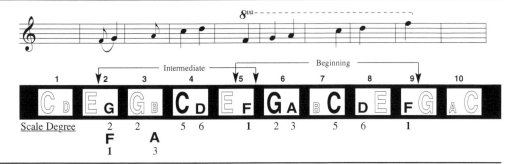

F Major Blues Scale

F Major Blues Scale:
F G A♭ A C D F
1 2 ♭3 3 5 6 1

- The F major blues scale is also known as the "bluegrass run."

- The following scale requires bending to the ♭3 blue note.

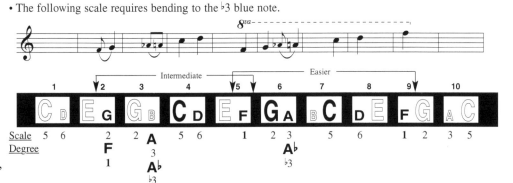

Playing F Blues

- Use your C harp to play blues in F.
- Resolve the V chord (C) on any C note.

When playing the F major blues scale you can effectively use all ten holes. Bend from the major 3rd (A) to the minor 3rd (A♭) in holes 3 and 6. Blow bend between the C and ~B notes in hole 7. The root F-A dyad can be drawn in holes 5–6 and 9–10. Draw bend between the F and ~E notes in hole 5. Draw bend to B♭ in hole 3.

Key of F
12-bar Blues Chord Progression:

F—	F—	F—	F—
1 2 3 4 •	1 2 3 4 •	1 2 3 4 •	1 2 3 4
B♭—	B♭—	F—	F—
1 2 3 4 •	1 2 3 4 •	1 2 3 4 •	1 2 3 4
C—	B♭—	F—	C—
1 2 3 4 •	1 2 3 4 •	1 2 3 4 •	1 2 3 4

(Each chord is played four beats.)

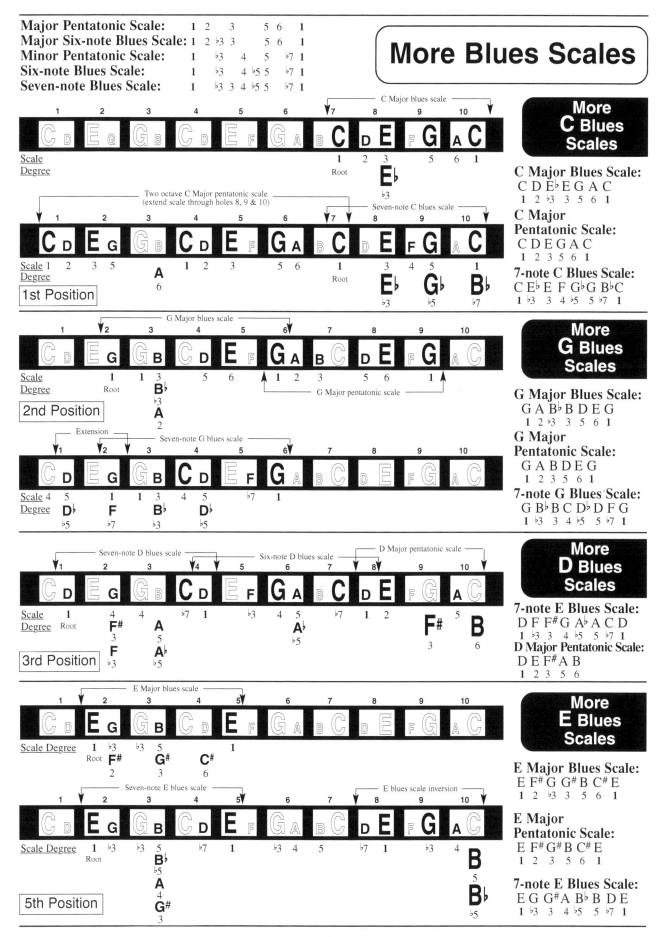

Major Pentatonic Scale: 1 2 3 5 6 1
Major Six-note Blues Scale: 1 2 ♭3 3 5 6 1
Minor Pentatonic Scale: 1 ♭3 4 5 ♭7 1
Six-note Blues Scale: 1 ♭3 4 ♭5 5 ♭7 1
Seven-note Blues Scale: 1 ♭3 3 4 ♭5 5 ♭7 1

More Blues Scales

More C Blues Scales

C Major Blues Scale:
C D E♭ E G A C
1 2 ♭3 3 5 6 1

C Major Pentatonic Scale:
C D E G A C
1 2 3 5 6 1

7-note C Blues Scale:
C E♭ E F G♭G B♭ C
1 ♭3 3 4 ♭5 5 ♭7 1

More G Blues Scales

G Major Blues Scale:
G A B♭ B D E G
1 2 ♭3 3 5 6 1

G Major Pentatonic Scale:
G A B D E G
1 2 3 5 6 1

7-note G Blues Scale:
G B♭ B C D♭ D F G
1 ♭3 3 4 ♭5 5 ♭7 1

More D Blues Scales

7-note E Blues Scale:
D F F# G A♭ A C D
1 ♭3 3 4 ♭5 5 ♭7 1

D Major Pentatonic Scale:
D E F# A B
1 2 3 5 6

More E Blues Scales

E Major Blues Scale:
E F# G G# B C# E
1 2 ♭3 3 5 6 1

E Major Pentatonic Scale:
E F# G# B C# E
1 2 3 5 6 1

7-note E Blues Scale:
E G G#A B♭ B D E
1 ♭3 3 4 ♭5 5 ♭7 1

21

Shakes, Tongue Slaps and Lifts

Shaking Trills

The shake is where you move or "shake" the harmonica back and forth in your mouth while keeping your head in a stable position to play two single notes in rapid succession. The straw or curled tongue method may also be used to shake a two-note trill.

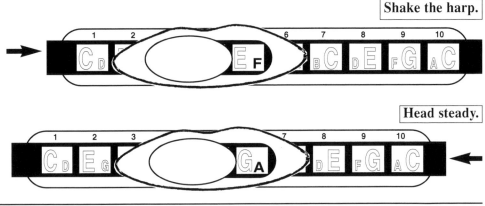

Shake the harp.

Head steady.

Head Shaking Trills

This is where you hold the harp steady and shake your head back and forth to play rapid, successive single notes. Trills can be executed while either blowing or drawing air. Some players prefer to shake both the harp and their head, instead of one or the other.

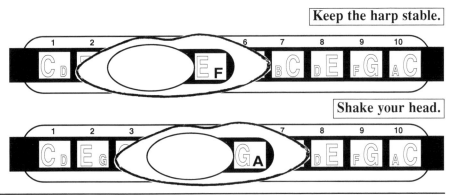

Keep the harp stable.

Shake your head.

Single, Double and Triple Hole Tongue Slaps

Pick either one, two or three holes. Cover them with your tongue after playing a chord, while allowing a single note to sound after you slap your tongue on the mouthpiece. Cover the holes either to the left or right of the single note.
Tongue Lift This is what it's called when you pull your tongue back away from the mouthpiece.

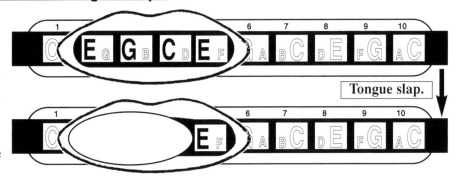

Tongue slap.

Curled Tongue Chord Slap

Use this technique to enhance your curled tongue melody playing. As you play single note melodies, periodically and rhythmically pull your tongue away from the mouthpiece, allowing a three-hole chord to play. Then return to the single note curled tongue position and the single note melody. Do a tongue lift and slap again. Align this combination of techniques with the rhythm of a tune to bring added depth and a bigger sound.

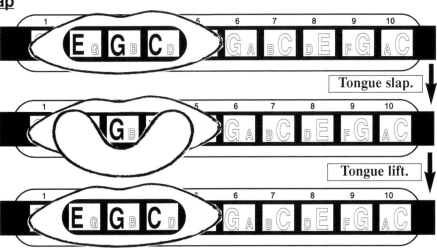

Tongue slap.

Tongue lift.

Playing Two Notes at the Same Time

Pursed Lip or Pucker Method Without using your tongue, blow or draw in two adjacent holes. You can also bend two notes at the same time. Draw bend minor thirds to get the "train horn" sound.

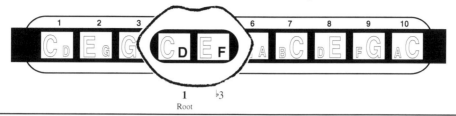

Single-hole Tongue Block Try different combinations by blocking a single hole with your tongue and sounding the notes on either side. The single hole tongue block is one way to play the F-A interval when an F chord is needed.

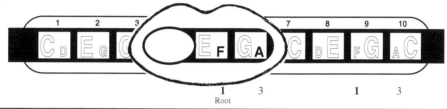

Single-hole Split Tongue Block Try different partial chord combinations all along the mouthpiece by blocking a single hole with your tongue and sounding the notes on either side. The single hole tongue block is a good way to play the D-A draw interval when you need to play along with a D major or D minor chord.

Two-hole Split Tongue Block Octaves

You can play octaves using the split tongue block method. There will also be times when you'll need to play a chord and you might only find one note in the chord available. Play it as an octave. For example, tongue block to play E octaves instead of using an E major arpeggio. Use root octaves as a substitute for any major or minor chord.
• **Three-hole split tongue block:** This is used for draw octaves B, D, F and A in holes 3 and above.

Two-hole Split Tongue Block for the Fat Sound

To get the "fat sound," your mouth and tongue should be in the same position as the octave two-hole tongue block, but you'll be playing two notes that are not octaves. If you draw in holes 3 and 6 (B and A), for example, you will hear what's called the fat sound. It's the root and the ♭7 sound creating tension. The draw G-F (holes 2 and 5) combination is popular among blues players in second position.

Building Chords

Chords
Chords are three or more notes sounded at the same time or functioning as if sounded at the same time.

Chord Construction
Triads are three-note chords built with adjacent thirds. When you add the 7th to a triad you get the four-note 7th chord. The notes beyond the 7th degree of the scale are called the upper extensions. The example below shows how triads are constructed in the key of C.

		C Major scale:	C	D	E	F	G	A	B	C D E F
Tonic or Root	**I**	**C Major chord:**	C		E		G			
	ii	**D minor chord:**		D		F		A		
	iii	**E minor chord:**			E		G		B	
subdominant	**IV**	**F Major chord:**				F		A		C
Dominant	**V**	**G Major chord:**					G		B	D
	vi	**A minor chord:**						A		C	E
	vii	**B diminished triad:**							B		D	F

12-bar Blues Chord Progression Formula:

I — I — I — I —
1 2 3 4 • 1 2 3 4 • 1 2 3 4 • 1 2 3 4
IV— IV— I — I —
1 2 3 4 • 1 2 3 4 • 1 2 3 4 • 1 2 3 4
V— VI—I — V —
1 2 3 4 • 1 2 3 4 • 1 2 3 4 • 1 2 3 4

This is the foundation for the blues progressions seen on pages 14–20.

Spelling Chords
Extended chords are built by taking every other note in the major scale through two octaves.

C Major scale:	C	D	E	F	G	A	B	C	D	E	F	G	A	B
Scale Degree	1		3		5		7		9		11		13		1

• **Minor Chord Family**: Flat the 3rd ($\flat$3) degree of the major scale.
• **Dominant Seventh Chord Family**: Flat the 7th ($\flat$7) degree of the major scale. When you see a chord with a "7" or any chord with a number higher than 7, it's always considered to have a $\flat$7 unless otherwise indicated.

Chord Name and Symbol	Scale Degrees	Chord Name and Symbol	Scale Degrees
Major ( ) (M)	1-3-5	**Add Nine** (add9)	1-3-5-9
Minor (m)	1-$\flat$3-5	**Six Nine** (6/9)	1-3-5-6-9
Suspended Second (sus2)	1-2-5	**Eleven** (11) (dom11)	1-3-5-$\flat$7-9-11
Suspended Fourth (sus4)	1-4-5	**Major Eleven** (Δ11) (M11) (Maj11)	1-3-5-7-9-11
Major Sixth (6)	1-3-5-6	**Minor Eleven** (m11)	1-$\flat$3-5-$\flat$7-9-11
Minor Sixth (m6)	1-$\flat$3-5-6	**Add Eleven** (add11)	1-3-5-11
Dominant Seventh (7) ($\flat$7) (dom7)	1-3-5-$\flat$7	**Thirteen** (13) (dom13)	1-3-5-$\flat$7-9-(11)-13
Major Seventh (Δ7) (M7) (Maj7)	1-3-5-7	**Major Thirteen** (Δ13) (M13) (Maj13)	1-3-5-7-9-(11)-13
Minor Seventh (m7)	1-$\flat$3-5-$\flat$7	**Minor Thirteen** (m13)	1-$\flat$3-5-$\flat$7-9-(11)-13
Ninth (9) (dom9)	1-3-5-$\flat$7-9	**Diminished** (°) (dim)	1-$\flat$3-$\flat$5-$\flat\flat$7
Major Ninth (Δ9) (M9) (Maj9)	1-3-5-7-9	**Half Diminished** (ø) (half dim) (m7$\flat$5)	1-$\flat$3-$\flat$5-$\flat$7
Minor Ninth (m9)	1-$\flat$3-5-$\flat$7-9	**Augmented Fifth** (#5) (aug5) (+5)	1-3-#5

Inversions

C Chord Inversions

Root Position: **CEG**
1st Inversion: **EGC**
2nd Inversion: **GCE**

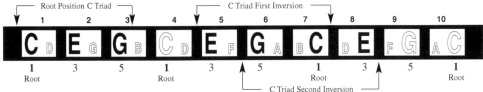

Chord Inversions ... for variety
The C major triad is spelled CEG. Play any EGC or GCE. Each is still a C chord but they are played with a different note in the bass. These are called inversions. Blow into holes 1, 2 and 3 (CEG) at the same time. This is called the root position C triad. It's when the root of the chord is the lowest note. Blow into holes 2, 3 and 4 (EGC) at the same time. That's still a C chord, but the 3rd of the C chord is its lowest note, giving it a different sound. This is called the 1st inversion. Now, blow into holes 3, 4 and 5 (GCE). You'll hear an even different sound. It's still a C chord, but it's the 2nd inversion of the C chord. The 2nd inversion has the 5th degree of the major scale as its lowest note.

Voicings

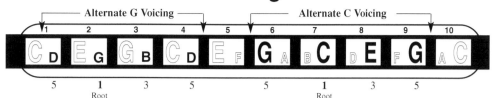

Voicings ... for richness

By duplicating and rearranging the notes in a chord, you can create new voicings that add flavor to your tone.

A "G" chord is spelled GBD. A common alternate voicing of the G chord, on the C harmonica, is DGBD.

A "C" chord is spelled CEG. One alternate voicing of the C chord is GCEG. Double up on the root (CEGC) or thirds (EGCE). Doubling the 5th and having that extra G in the bass enriches the sound of the C chord. Try blowing CEGCE. You can also use any other combination of C, E or G notes when blowing the C chord to create various alternate voicings.

Chord Substitutions • Playing Intervals • Dyads

Faking Major and Minor Chords

Although bending your way through single note melodies is an exciting and rewarding pursuit in itself, the music can be even more interesting when you insert chords into the melody. Since there is only one blow chord and a handful of draw chords built into a diatonic harmonica, one way to achieve this is by playing intervals, or "faking" major and minor chords. This is done by playing only two notes of a chord at a time. These are called dyads. They're sometimes referred to as double-stops, partial chords or intervals.

The root and the 5th degree.

The minor and major value of any chord is determined by the third degree of the scale—more specifically, whether it has a flat third or not. Minor chords have a minor third (♭3) and major chords have a major third (3). By only using the root (1) and the fifth (5) of a chord, you can emulate or fake either a major or a minor chord, because there's no third to define its major or minor characteristic.

Example: Let's say you're playing a tune that has a Cm chord and you're using your C major diatonic harp. You can blow any of the G-C (5th-root) combinations (holes 3 and 4, 6 and 7 or 9 and 10) to emulate or fake the Cm chord. When you're playing these two-note intervals, you don't have to think about whether musicians are going to play a major or a minor chord because you're only playing the root and the 5th. Chances are, the guitarist or the keyboard player will be playing the minor third, so the need to play the 3rd isn't crucial in those situations. (See Dyad, page 26)

The root and the 3rd, or 3rd and the 5th degree.

Also, there will be times when you will want to play a chord and a triad won't be an option due to the arrangement of notes on the harmonica. You can play any two notes of the chord—the root and the 3rd, or the 3rd and the 5th. In this situation, you do have to play the appropriate major or minor third (3 or ♭3). Any two notes played together can "imply" a chord or chord extension.

Pursed Lip F Dyad

Tongue Block F Dyad

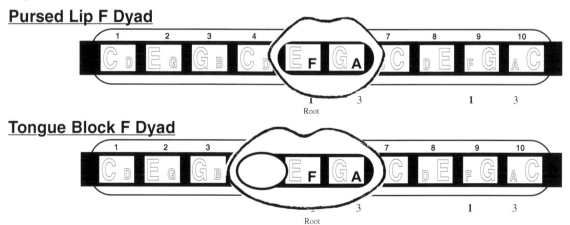

Using Intervals as Chord Substitutes

1) For blues in the key of C, the F-A interval or trill can be substituted for the IV chord (F). Also, try a three-hole F octave tongue block. (See the 12-bar C blues progression, page 14.)

2) For blues in the key of G, the D-A single-hole split tongue block interval illustrated on page 23 can be used as a substitute for the V chord (D). Also try a D octave three-hole trill or a two-hole or three-hole D octave tongue block. (Refer to the 12-bar G blues progression on page 15.)

THE BLOW CHORD

C Major Chord

C (CEG).   (I)
- For C root positions and inversions, blow in any three adjacent holes.
- Blow four or more holes for voicings.

Blow Dyad

C or Cm (GC).
- Blow any G-C pairs.

DRAW CHORDS

G Major Chord

G (GBD).   (V)
- Draw in holes 2, 3 and 4 only.

G (DGBD). Use the additional D (5th) as the bass note.

G7 Chord

G7 (GBDF).
- Draw holes 2–5.

G7 (DGBDF). This voicing uses a double 5th—a D in the bass.

G9 Chord

G9 (GBDFA).
- Can you stretch your mouth over six holes? Try a voicing with double 5ths—a D in the bass.

Draw Dyads

Gm or G (D-G).
- Draw 1 and 2 or tongue block center hole 3 for (G-D).

D or Dm (D-A).
- Tongue block center hole 5 (F) and draw holes 4 and 6.

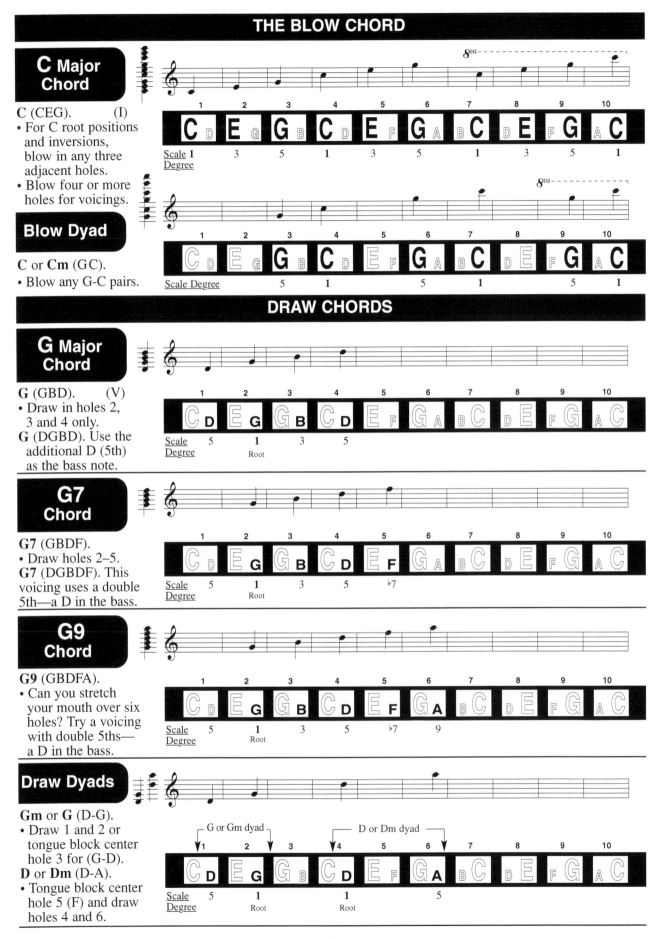

26

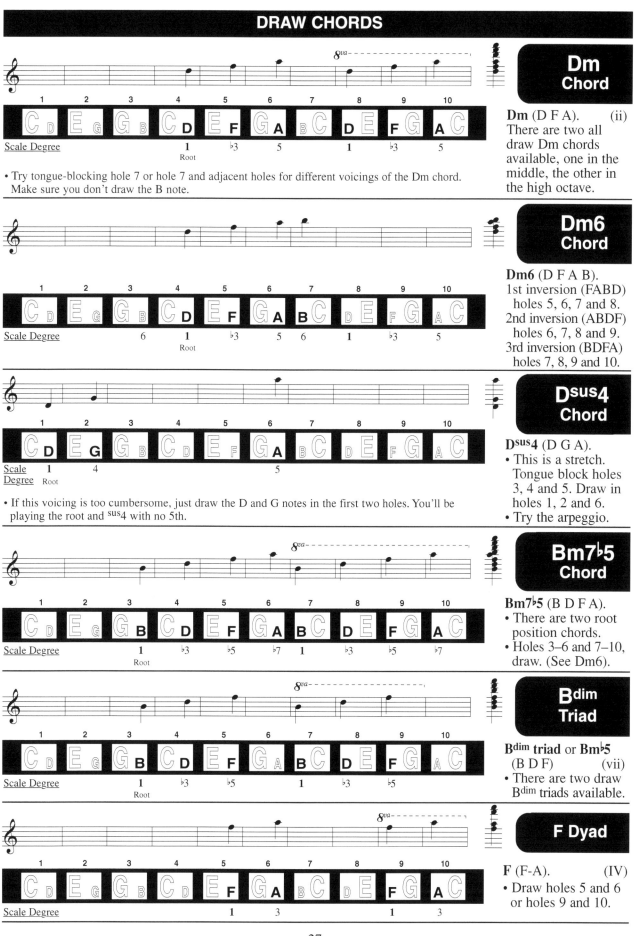

Dm Chord

Dm (D F A). (ii)
There are two all draw Dm chords available, one in the middle, the other in the high octave.

• Try tongue-blocking hole 7 or hole 7 and adjacent holes for different voicings of the Dm chord. Make sure you don't draw the B note.

Dm6 Chord

Dm6 (D F A B).
1st inversion (FABD) holes 5, 6, 7 and 8.
2nd inversion (ABDF) holes 6, 7, 8 and 9.
3rd inversion (BDFA) holes 7, 8, 9 and 10.

Dsus4 Chord

Dsus4 (D G A).
• This is a stretch. Tongue block holes 3, 4 and 5. Draw in holes 1, 2 and 6.
• Try the arpeggio.

• If this voicing is too cumbersome, just draw the D and G notes in the first two holes. You'll be playing the root and sus4 with no 5th.

Bm7♭5 Chord

Bm7♭5 (B D F A).
• There are two root position chords.
• Holes 3–6 and 7–10, draw. (See Dm6).

Bdim Triad

Bdim triad or **Bm♭5** (B D F) (vii)
• There are two draw Bdim triads available.

F Dyad

F (F-A). (IV)
• Draw holes 5 and 6 or holes 9 and 10.

Getting the Most Out of the Arpeggios

Arpeggios ... to Expand the Chord Pool

Arpeggios are chords played one note at a time in sequence, normally from lowest to highest. It's certainly acceptable to play the notes in an order other than from lowest to highest. Even though some arpeggios on the C harp require you to only blow (the C chord) or only draw (the G, G7, Dm etc.), the majority require you to do both. This takes a little more concentration, but knowing where to find arpeggios comes in handy when you need to play a normally-elusive chord. The arpeggios shown in this book all have one thing in common—they can be played somewhere on the harp without bending or overbending. Arpeggios that can be played with bends are shown with and without bends, to accommodate both beginning and intermediate players.

Bending and Overbending

By including bending and overbending, you can play any and every chord as an arpeggio on your 10-hole C diatonic harp. While it is certainly possible to play a D♭ arpeggio (D♭ F A♭) on a C harp, it's a lot easier to just play it as an all blow chord on a D♭ harp. There are also instances where a tune or musical phrase modulates a 1/2 step, perhaps two or three times in a row. That's where knowing how to arpeggiate your way through the changes on one harp can be invaluable. To build arpeggios with overbends, use your knowledge of chord construction and the overbending chart on page 9. In addition to the examples shown in this section, you can also use the major scale charts on pages 38–41 to help you build any arpeggios you might need. Practice hitting the notes you need to bend to, exactly—without adjusting the pitch or until you finally play it without sliding into it. Get to know the shape that your tongue and mouth need to be in, in order to achieve the desired pre-bent note. Remember it. Make the shape, then release the flow of air.

For Beginning and Intermediate Level Players

Generally, the easiest configuration of arpeggios appear in the upper two octaves without bending. Many of the arpeggios in the lower octave use draw bends which add color and feeling to a piece, but require a little more practice to execute and master. Some arpeggios have blow bends in the upper octave.

Example: F arpeggio

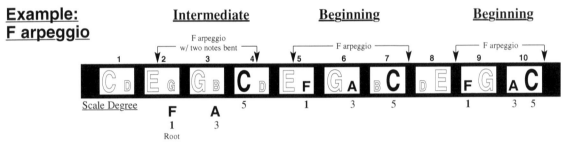

Brackets Highlight Suggested Arpeggios

The arpeggios shown in brackets are suggested and have a triad in the root position. I encourage you to try different inversions and voicings found outside of the brackets. Many times, in the lower octave, the root is a note that must be pre-bent. Try variations that blend with the melody and chord structure of the tune you're working on. Use the arpeggio section as a reference guide. When you run across a piece of music that has a chord you need to use, find it in this section and play it as an arpeggio.

Scale Degree Numbers

Throughout this section, the root will be labeled with either a bold (**1**) under it or the word "root." The scale degrees for all available notes in the arpeggio that don't require bending are labeled under the graphic. This gives you the opportunity to explore voicings other than the ones suggested in brackets. In practice, the voicing you use will be guided by the nature of the tune and where the melody is coming from and going to. There are many voicings and inversions other than the examples suggested in brackets. Explore each arpeggio by playing the numbered scale degree notes outside of the brackets, too.

Utilizing Arpeggios and the Essence of Melody

Melodies can be created by intermingling bits and pieces of scales and arpeggios. By meshing arpeggios with scales and modes and then integrating them, you can make a melody of your own. Blend arpeggios with modes seamlessly. Repeating, bending and holding notes are all part of the bag of tricks you can draw from.

Remember: The following suggested arpeggios were chosen because they can be played somewhere on the C diatonic harmonica without bending a note. Experiment with bending and alternate voicings.

• To play the A arpeggios in the lower octave, draw the root A note pre-bent.

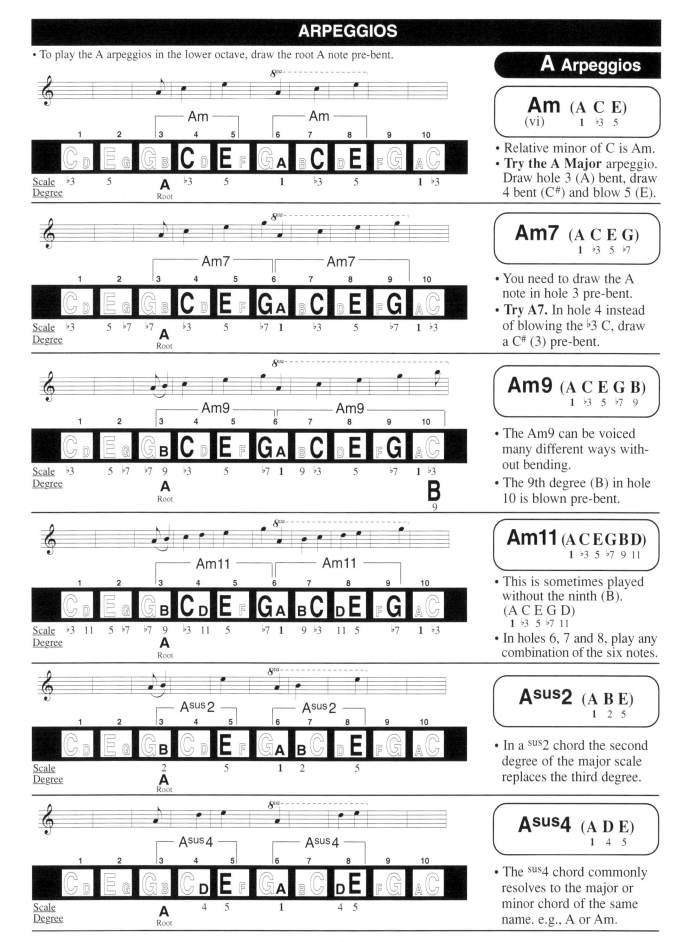

A Arpeggios

Am (A C E)
(vi)   1 ♭3 5

• Relative minor of C is Am.
• **Try the A Major** arpeggio. Draw hole 3 (A) bent, draw 4 bent (C#) and blow 5 (E).

Am7 (A C E G)
1 ♭3 5 ♭7

• You need to draw the A note in hole 3 pre-bent.
• **Try A7.** In hole 4 instead of blowing the ♭3 C, draw a C# (3) pre-bent.

Am9 (A C E G B)
1 ♭3 5 ♭7 9

• The Am9 can be voiced many different ways without bending.
• The 9th degree (B) in hole 10 is blown pre-bent.

Am11 (A C E G B D)
1 ♭3 5 ♭7 9 11

• This is sometimes played without the ninth (B). (A C E G D)
1 ♭3 5 ♭7 11
• In holes 6, 7 and 8, play any combination of the six notes.

Asus2 (A B E)
1 2 5

• In a sus2 chord the second degree of the major scale replaces the third degree.

Asus4 (A D E)
1 4 5

• The sus4 chord commonly resolves to the major or minor chord of the same name. e.g., A or Am.

C Arpeggios

• The G notes in hole 2 draw and hole 3 blow are identical. This gives you a chance to catch your breath by either blowing or drawing. Use the most convenient one.

C (C E G)
(I) 1 3 5

• It's the chord you heard when you blew on a C harmonica for the first time and you'll find the C chord everywhere you blow.

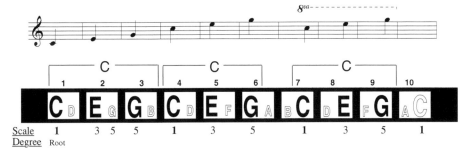

C^Maj7 (C E G B)
1 3 5 △7

• You'll find the C^Maj7 in all of the octaves. In the highest octave bend to the B note in hole 10.
• The symbol for the 7th degree of the major scale is (△7).

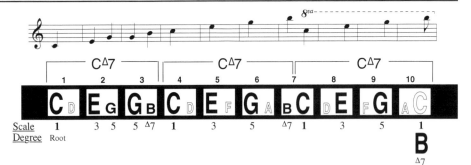

C^Maj9 (C E G B D)
1 3 5 △7 9

• You'll find the C^Maj9 in both the middle and lower octaves.
• For an alternate voicing, try the draw D (9), in hole number 4.

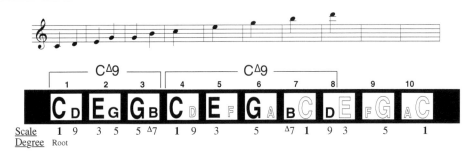

C^Maj11 (CEGBDF)
1 3 5 △7 9 11

• With this arpeggio, play all the reeds but the A notes.
• There is another C^Maj11 in holes 4–9.
• Sometimes played without the 9th. (1, 3, 5, △7, 11).

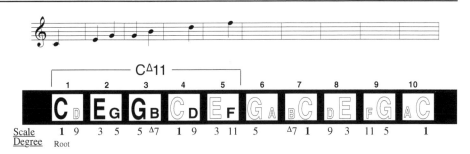

C^Maj13 (CEGBDFA)
1 3 5 △7 9 11 13

• When played on other instruments as a chord, normally the 11th is omitted. (1, 3, 5, △7, 9, 13).
• Played as an arpeggio, the 11th acts as a melodic passing tone and its use is acceptable.

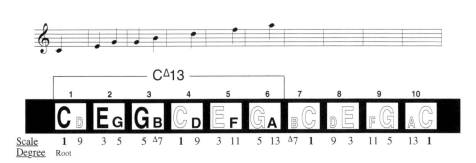

ARPEGGIOS

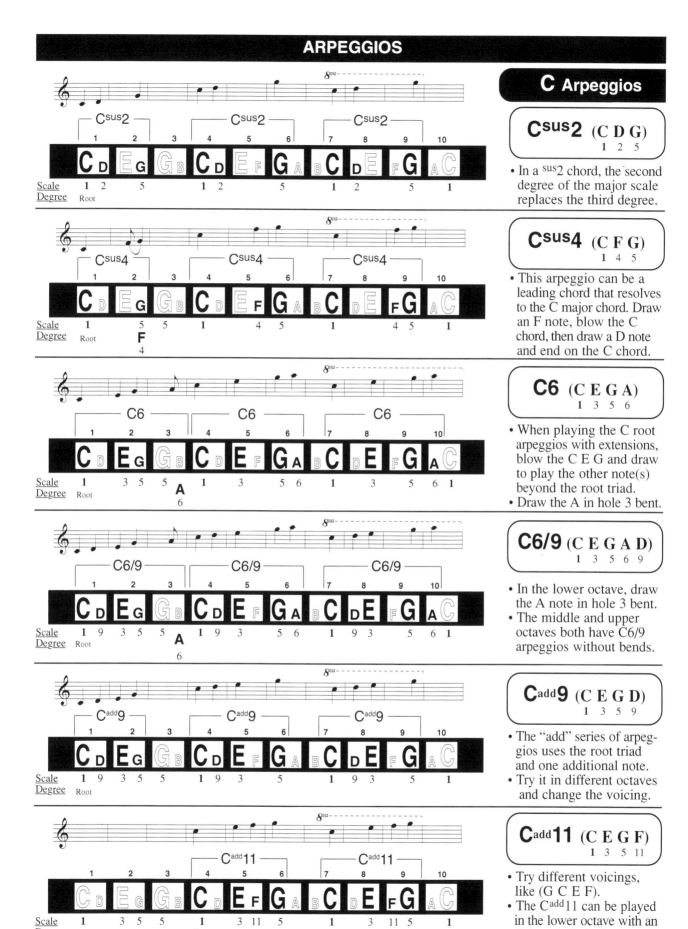

31

D Arpeggios

• To play the lower octave Dm arpeggios, draw the F and A notes pre-bent.

Dm (D F A)
(ii)   1 ♭3 5

• **Try D Major** (D F♯A).
  1 3 5
• The D major arpeggio can be played by bending to an F♯, instead of playing the ♭3 F, in holes 2 and 9.

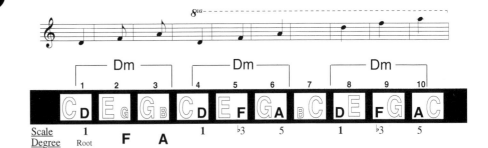

Dm7 (D F A C)
1 ♭3 5 ♭7

• **Try D7** (DF♯AC).
  1 3 5 ♭7
• The D7 arpeggio can be played by bending to an F♯, instead of playing the ♭3 F, in holes 2 and 9.

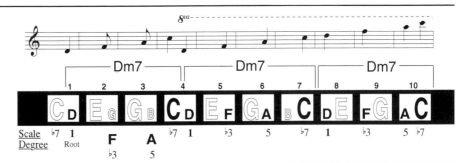

Dm9 (D F A C E)
1 ♭3 5 ♭7 9

• **Try D9** (DF♯ACE).
  1 3 5 ♭7 9
• Play the D9 arpeggio by drawing to a bent F♯, instead of the bent ♭3 F in hole 2.

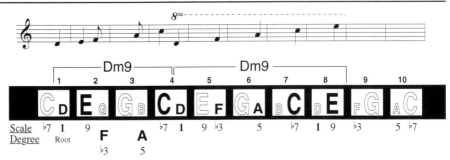

Dm11 (DFACEG)
1 ♭3 5 ♭7 9 11

• Can be played without the 9th. (D F A C G).
  1 ♭3 5 ♭7 11
• **Try D11** (DF♯ACEG).
  1 3 5 ♭7 9 11
• The D11 arpeggio can be played by bending to an F♯, instead of F, in hole 2.

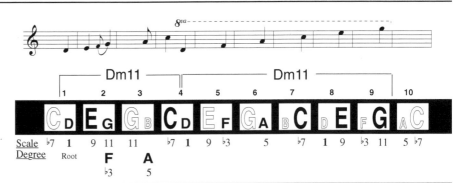

Dm13 (DFACEGB)
1 ♭3 5 ♭7 9 11 13

• Can be played without the 9th and/or the 11th.

• **Try the D13** (DF♯ACEGB).
  1 3 5 ♭7 9 11 13
• The D13 arpeggio is played by draw bending to an F♯, instead of F, in hole 2.

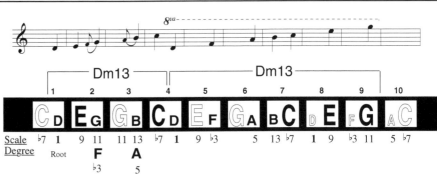

D Arpeggios

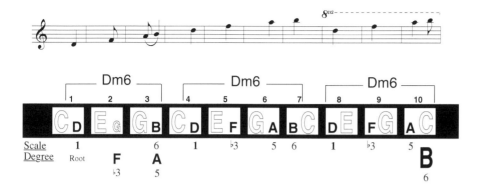

Dm6 (D F A B)
1 ♭3 5 6

- This Dm6 can be played as a straight draw chord in the middle octave.
- **Try D6** (D F# A B).
  1 3 5 6
- The D6 arpeggio can be played by drawing an F# in hole 2 bent or blowing an F# bent in hole 9, instead of drawing the ♭3 F note.

• Blow the B note in the high octave pre-bent.

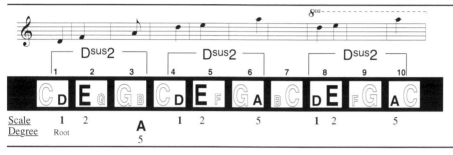

Dsus2 (D E A)
1 2 5

- Draw the lower octave A note in hole 3 pre-bent.
- Try different octaves and inversions.

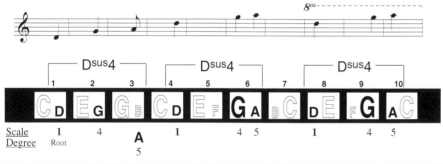

Dsus4 (D G A)
1 4 5

- Draw the lower octave A note in hole 3 pre-bent.
- In the sus4 chord, the fourth degree of the major scale replaces the third degree.
- Try different octaves and inversions.

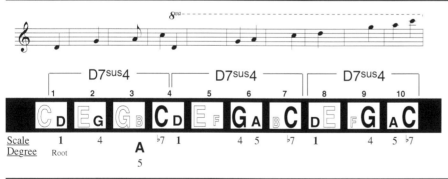

D7sus4 (D G A C)
1 4 5 ♭7

- The D7sus4 chord can be used as a substitute for, or in conjunction with, a Dsus4 chord and can add character to a musical phrase.
- In hole 3, draw the lower octave A note pre-bent.

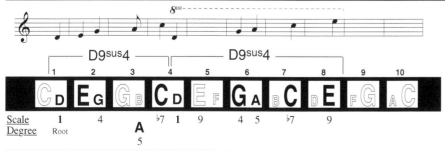

D9sus4 (D G A C E)
1 4 5 ♭7 9

- The easiest version is found in the middle of the harmonica.
- In hole 3, draw the lower octave A note pre-bent.

E Arpeggios

Em (E G B)
(iii)   1 ♭3 5

- **Try E Major** (E G#B).
  1 3 5
- The E major arpeggio can be played by drawing a G# bent in holes 3 or 6 instead of playing the ♭3 G.

• The G notes in hole 2 draw and hole 3 blow are identical. Use the most convenient one.

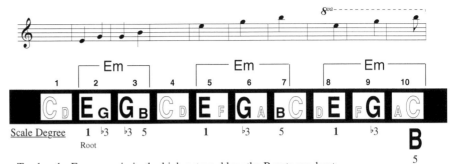

• To play the Em arpeggio in the high octave, blow the B note pre-bent.

Em7 (E G B D)
1 ♭3 5 ♭7

- **Try E7** (E G#B D).
  1 3 5 ♭7
- The E7 arpeggio can be played by drawing a G# bent in holes 3 or 6 instead of playing the ♭3 G.

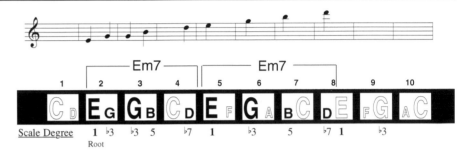

Em11 (E G B D A)
1 ♭3 5 ♭7 11

- **Try E11** (E G#B D A).
  1 3 5 ♭7 11
- The E11 arpeggio can be played by drawing a G# bent in holes 3 or 6 instead of playing the ♭3 G.

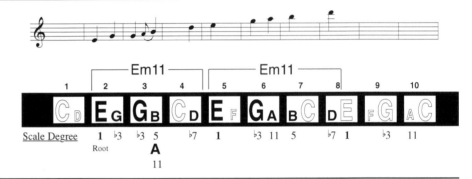

Esus4 (E A B)
1 sus4 5

- The sus4 chord commonly resolves to the major or minor chord of the same name—in this case an E major or E minor arpeggio.
- In hole 10, blow the B note pre-bent.

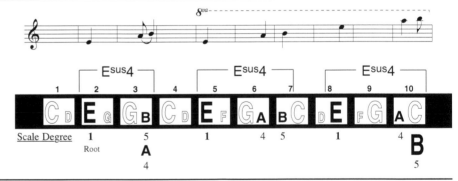

E7sus4 (E A B D)
1 sus4 5 ♭7

- The E7sus4 chord can be used as a substitute for, or in conjunction with, the Esus4 chord and can add more character to a musical phrase.

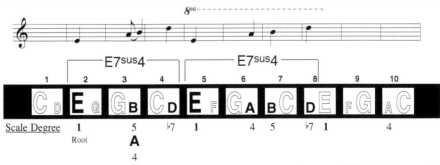

• To play the F arpeggios on the lower end of the harp, draw the F and A notes pre-bent.

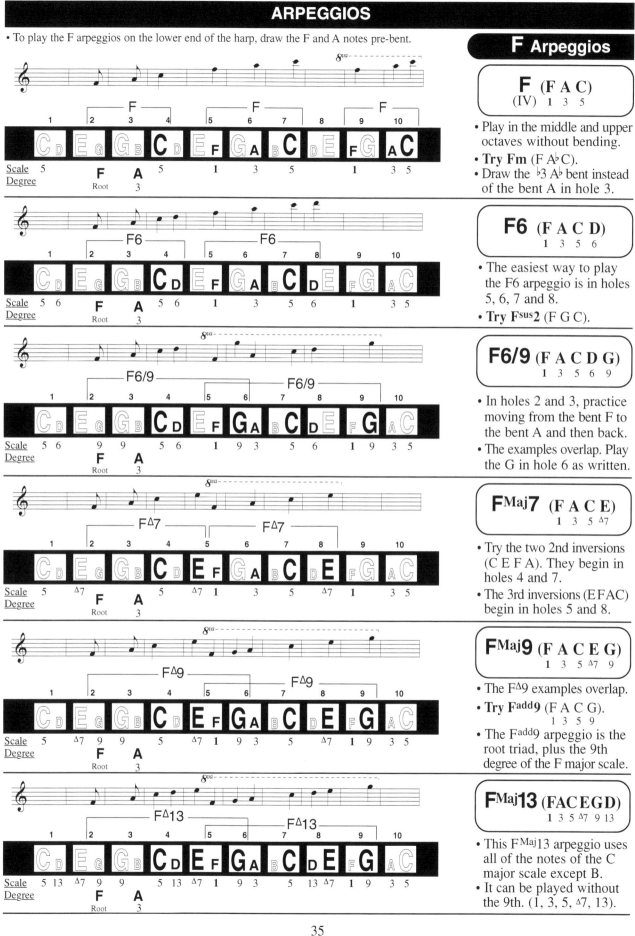

F (F A C)
(IV) 1 3 5

• Play in the middle and upper octaves without bending.
• **Try Fm** (F A♭ C).
• Draw the ♭3 A♭ bent instead of the bent A in hole 3.

F6 (F A C D)
1 3 5 6

• The easiest way to play the F6 arpeggio is in holes 5, 6, 7 and 8.
• **Try Fsus2** (F G C).

F6/9 (F A C D G)
1 3 5 6 9

• In holes 2 and 3, practice moving from the bent F to the bent A and then back.
• The examples overlap. Play the G in hole 6 as written.

FMaj7 (F A C E)
1 3 5 △7

• Try the two 2nd inversions (C E F A). They begin in holes 4 and 7.
• The 3rd inversions (E F A C) begin in holes 5 and 8.

FMaj9 (F A C E G)
1 3 5 △7 9

• The F△9 examples overlap.
• **Try Fadd9** (F A C G).
   1 3 5 9
• The Fadd9 arpeggio is the root triad, plus the 9th degree of the F major scale.

FMaj13 (F A C E G D)
1 3 5 △7 9 13

• This FMaj13 arpeggio uses all of the notes of the C major scale except B.
• It can be played without the 9th. (1, 3, 5, △7, 13).

35

G Arpeggios

• Holes 2 and 3 have the same G note—the root of the G chord. Both G notes are labeled "root" to remind you there's a choice. One is a draw G and the other one a blow G. Use the most convenient one.

G (G B D)
(V)   1   3   5

• **G** with a D bass adds a new dimension to the arpeggio. (D G B D).
• **Play Gm** (G B♭ D).
   1 ♭3 5
• In hole 3, instead of the B (3), draw a ♭3 B♭ pre-bent.

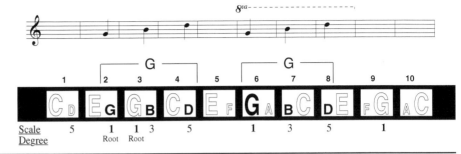

G7 (G B D F)
1   3   5   ♭7

• The G dominant 7th chord can be a good transitional tool when used after a G chord, just before moving to a C chord.

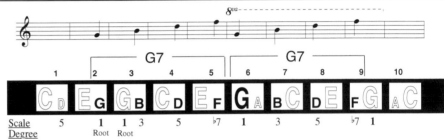

G9 (G B D F A)
1   3   5   ♭7   9

• **G9** has a root triad, ♭7 and 9.
• **G**add9 (G B D A).
       1 3 5 9
• The G add9 arpeggio is the root triad plus the 9th degree of the G major scale.

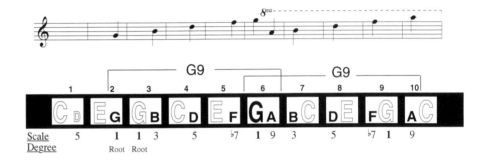

G11 (G B D F A C)
1   3   5   ♭7   9   11

• Can be played without the 9th. (1, 3, 5, ♭7, 11).
• **G**add11 (G B D C).
         1 3 5 11
• The G add11 arpeggio is the root triad plus the 11th degree of the G major scale.

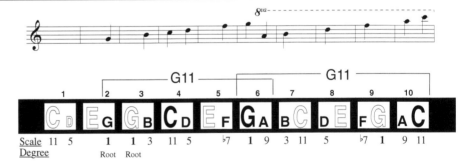

G13 (G B D F A C E)
1   3   5   ♭7   9   11 13

• When played on other instruments as a chord (all of the notes at the same time), normally the 11th is omitted. (1, 3, 5, ♭7, 9, 13).
• Played as an arpeggio, the 11th acts as a melodic passing tone and its use is acceptable.

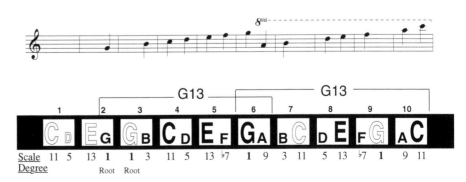

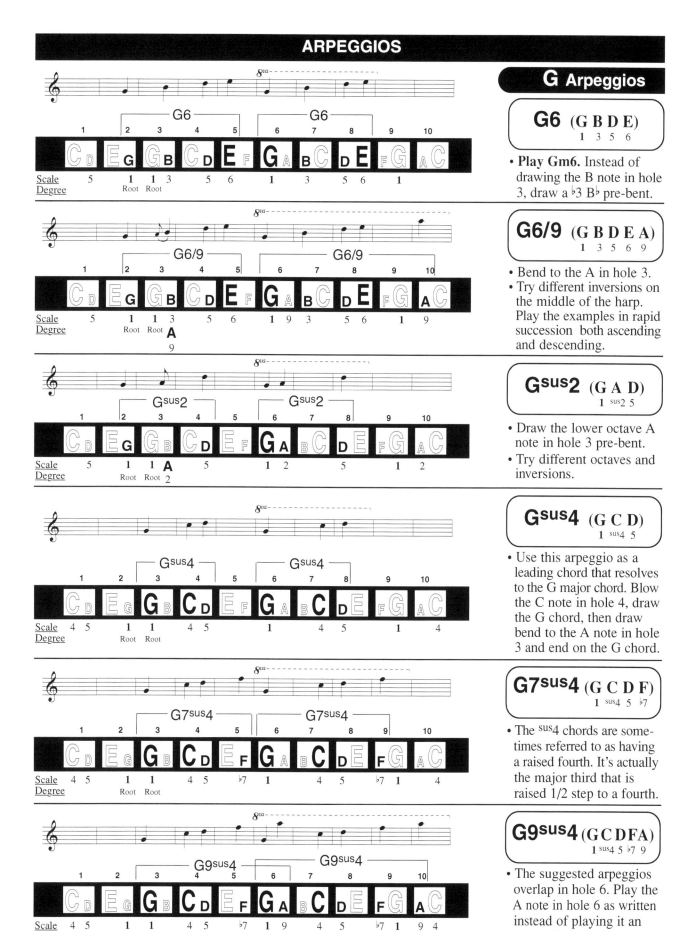

G Arpeggios

G6 (G B D E)
1 3 5 6

- **Play Gm6.** Instead of drawing the B note in hole 3, draw a ♭3 B♭ pre-bent.

G6/9 (G B D E A)
1 3 5 6 9

- Bend to the A in hole 3.
- Try different inversions on the middle of the harp. Play the examples in rapid succession both ascending and descending.

G sus2 (G A D)
1 sus2 5

- Draw the lower octave A note in hole 3 pre-bent.
- Try different octaves and inversions.

G sus4 (G C D)
1 sus4 5

- Use this arpeggio as a leading chord that resolves to the G major chord. Blow the C note in hole 4, draw the G chord, then draw bend to the A note in hole 3 and end on the G chord.

G7 sus4 (G C D F)
1 sus4 5 ♭7

- The sus4 chords are sometimes referred to as having a raised fourth. It's actually the major third that is raised 1/2 step to a fourth.

G9 sus4 (G C D F A)
1 sus4 5 ♭7 9

- The suggested arpeggios overlap in hole 6. Play the A note in hole 6 as written instead of playing it an octave higher.

Major Scales on the C Harp for Advanced Players

With the exception of the C major scale, all of the scales in this section require bending and/or overbending. Learning these scales will provide a foundation for you to build any chord and play it as an arpeggio on your C harp. Playing the major scales in keys other than C requires that you know how to overblow, overdraw and bend with great skill.

There will be times when playing the harmonica that you'll be in the right key, but the tune will momentarily stray from it. Then, suddenly, you'll feel like you've been left out in the cold. By referring to this section and learning the piece of music with its needed bends, overblows or overdraws, you'll be able to play your way through the changes that move outside of the key. Knowing how to find those "missing" notes on a harp in a particular key can be invaluable.

After playing through these examples (or attempting to), you'll find that it more than highlights the usefulness of owning diatonic harmonicas in many different keys. Although it might be easier to play a tune using two harmonicas in different keys, sometimes the right harps aren't within reach. If you can't hit the overbends—don't worry. It takes a long time for most people to master. It's a lot easier to play a B major scale on a harp in the key of B than it is on a C harp. This is not to overshadow the usefulness of knowing how to learn a single, seemingly difficult musical phrase in what might be an otherwise simple tune on one harmonica. There are phrasings that are defined by the available bends, unique to the Richter-style major diatonic harmonica. Some bend and overbend notes are easier than others to play on the C harp.

Although any standard diatonic harp can be used, there are some models that seem to lend themselves to overblowing. Hohner®'s Meisterklasse®, Golden Melody®, the Lee Oskar® and Suzuki Promaster® harps are among them. Suzuki® makes a model called the Overdrive® that is designed specifically to make overblowing more easily accessible.

Even after you become familiar with overbending, you'll probably agree, it's still easier to play certain scales and modes on a harmonica in the appropriate key. If you can currently overbend one or two notes, use it to your advantage. Work on the others. With practice, they will come in time.

Practice playing the scales ascending and then descending. All of the scales shown in this section are a minimum of two octaves and in the root position.

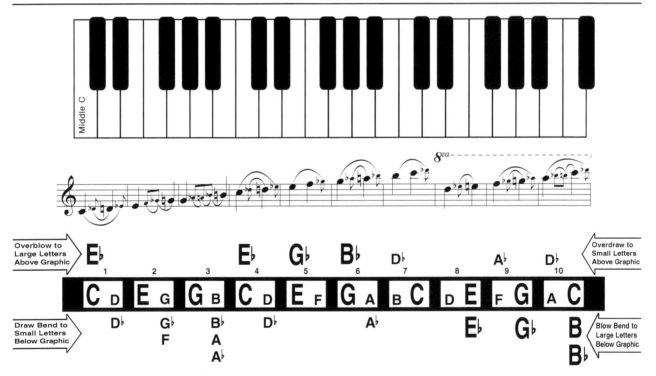

Visualize the Harmonica Chromatically To more easily visualize the diatonic harmonica chromatically for scale or chord construction, use a keyboard. It's linear and easier to comprehend. Then visualize the chromatic scale on the harmonica. Play the scales ascending, then descending. This will help you organize your harmonica playing in a more linear fashion.

When you play an overbend, refrain from sounding the reed note first. Position your tongue and mouth correctly before you attempt it. After much trial and error, you should be able to play the overbend without hitting the reed note first.

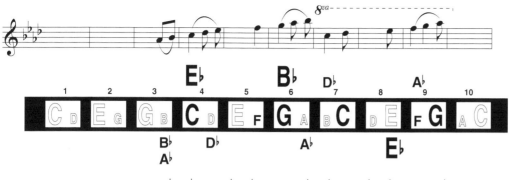

A♭ Major Scale

- Begins in hole 3 draw pre-bent.
- In hole 4, blow the C, draw the D♭ pre-bent, then overblow the E♭.
- In hole 6, blow the G, draw the A♭ pre-bent, then overblow the B♭.

Scale Degrees	A♭	B♭	C	D♭	E♭	F	G	A♭	B♭	C	D♭	E♭	F	G	A♭
	1	2	3	4	5	6	7	1	2	3	4	5	6	7	1

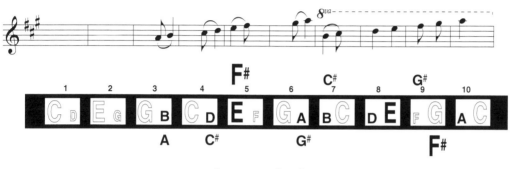

A Major Scale

- Begins in hole 3 draw pre-bent.
- In hole 9, blow the F# bent then overdraw the G#.
- One overblow.
- Two overdraws.
- Three draw bends.
- One blow bend.

Scale Degrees	A	B	C#	D	E	F#	G#	A	B	C#	D	E	F#	G#	A
	1	2	3	4	5	6	7	1	2	3	4	5	6	7	1

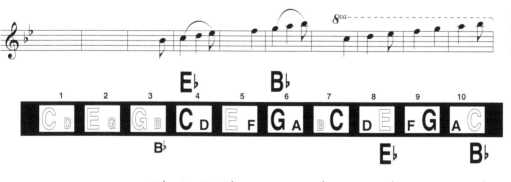

B♭ Major Scale

- Begins in hole 3 draw pre-bent.
- There is an E♭ and a B♭ overblow.
- Blow both the E♭ in hole 8 and the B♭ in hole 10 pre-bent.

Scale Degrees	B♭	C	D	E♭	F	G	A	B♭	C	D	E♭	F	G	A	B♭
	1	2	3	4	5	6	7	1	2	3	4	5	6	7	1

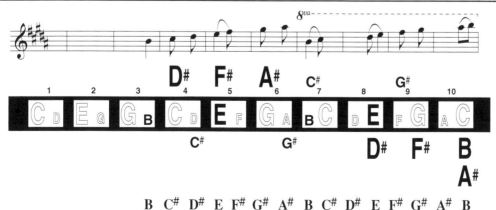

B Major Scale

- In hole 4, draw the C# bent, then overblow the D#.
- In hole 6, draw the G# bent, then overblow the A#.
- In hole 9, blow the F# bent, then overdraw the G#.

Scale Degrees	B	C#	D#	E	F#	G#	A#	B	C#	D#	E	F#	G#	A#	B
	1	2	3	4	5	6	7	1	2	3	4	5	6	7	1

C Major Scale

- Three octave scale.
- Three bends.
- No sharps.
- No flats.
- No overblows.
- No overdraws.

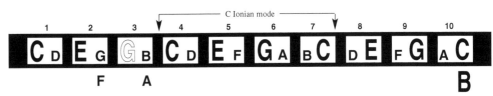

Scale	C	D	E	F	G	A	B	C	D	E	F	G	A	B	C	D	E	F	G	A	B	C
Degrees	1	2	3	4	5	6	7	1	2	3	4	5	6	7	1	2	3	4	5	6	7	1

D♭ Major Scale

- Three octave scale.
- Begins in hole 1 with the draw D♭ pre-bent.
- All notes except C and F are either overbent or bent notes.
- Use a D♭ harp instead. It's easier.

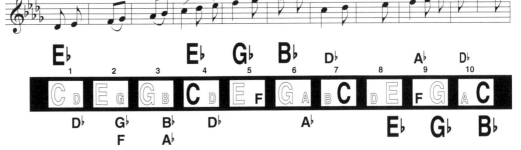

Scale Degrees	D♭	E♭	F	G♭	A♭	B♭	C	D♭	E♭	F	G♭	A♭	B♭	C	D♭	E♭	F	G♭	A♭	B♭	C	D♭
	1	2	3	4	5	6	7	1	2	3	4	5	6	7	1	2	3	4	5	6	7	1

D Major Scale

- The D major scale can be played on the lower end without overbends.
- One overblow.
- One overdraw.
- Three draw bends.

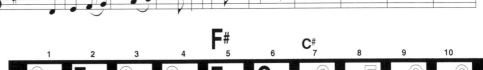

Scale Degrees	D	E	F#	G	A	B	C#	D	E	F#	G	A	B	C#	D
	1	2	3	4	5	6	7	1	2	3	4	5	6	7	1

E♭ Major Scale

- In hole 1, overblow the root E♭ bent.
- In hole 3, draw the A♭ and the B♭ bent.
- In hole 6, blow G, draw the A♭ bent, and overblow the B♭. In hole 8, blow the E♭ bent.

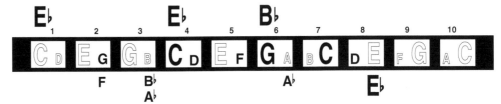

Scale	E♭	F	G	A♭	B♭	C	D	E♭	F	G	A♭	B♭	C	D	E♭
Degrees	1	2	3	4	5	6	7	1	2	3	4	5	6	7	1

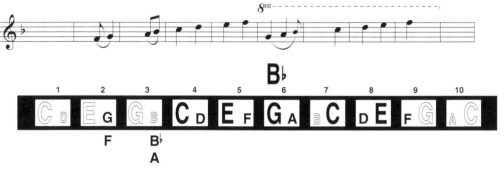

E
Major Scale

• Three notes of this scale are in hole 3.
• Draw the F# in hole 2 pre-bent.
• In hole 4, draw the C# bent, then overblow the D#.

F
Major Scale

• The F major scale can be played on the lower end without overbends.
• Begins in hole 2 draw pre-bent.
• In hole 3, draw the A and B♭ bent.

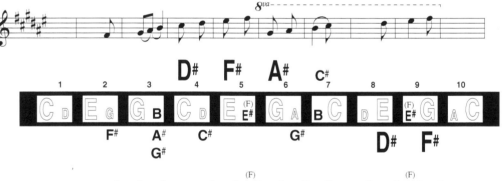

F#
Major Scale

• The F# major scale has an E#. The enharmonic equivalent of E# is F.
• Begins in hole 2 draw pre-bent.
• All notes except B and F are either overbent or bent.

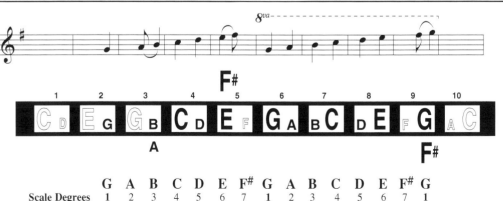

G
Major Scale

• The G major scale can be played on the high end without overbending.
• One draw bend.
• One overblow.
• One blow bend.

Extended Range C Diatonic Harmonicas

Hohner #364: In this 12-hole model, the C note in hole 1 is an octave below middle C. Additional notes in holes 11 and 12 are positioned to retain the integrity of the blow C chord while adding the draw B and D notes. This has a two octave C major scale. You can play two octave C Ionian, D Dorian, E Phrygian and B Locrian modes without bending.

Hohner #365: In this 14-hole, four-octave+ model, the first hole is an octave below middle C. It is the same as the #364 but with two additional holes—13 and 14. On this harp, all of the modes can played through two complete octaves without bending.

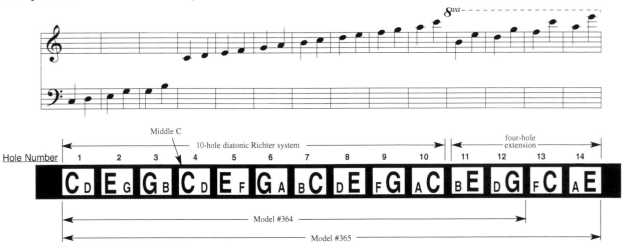

Extreme Bending C Diatonic Harmonica

Model XB40: Invented by Rick Epping and produced by Hohner®, this 10-hole, 40 reed Richter-style diatonic harmonica was designed to give the player a greater range of notes to bend. You can bend notes in all of the holes, regardless of whether you are blowing or drawing. All of the reed notes bend down two half steps except hole 3, where you can draw bend three half steps. This is achieved through valved tripartite air chambers. One blow and one draw reed chamber are separated by an internal valve chamber. Each reed chamber has a non-primary reed installed for the sole purpose of accommodating the bend. The potential interval of a bend is determined by the interval or musical distance between the pitch of the primary reed and the non-primary reed. Using this model eliminates the need to overbend. The range of this C harp is from B♭ below middle C to C—three octaves above middle C.

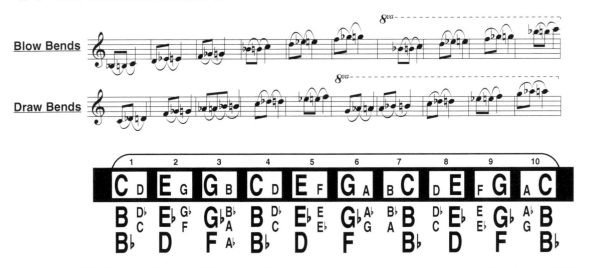

C Diatonic Harmonicas with a Slide Assembly

The Koch Chromatic® and the Slide Harp® are 10-hole major diatonic harmonicas using the Richter system. The feature that separates these models from other diatonic models is a slide that, when depressed, raises all the notes a half step which allows you to easily get those elusive E♭ notes in all three octaves. This is a C and a C♯ or D♭ diatonic harp all in one. There are 40 reeds total—20 in the key of C and 20 in the key of D♭/C♯. You can bend to the same intervals as you can on a D♭ harp when the plunger is depressed.

HOHNER®
#980/40
Koch®
#7312/40
Slide Harp®

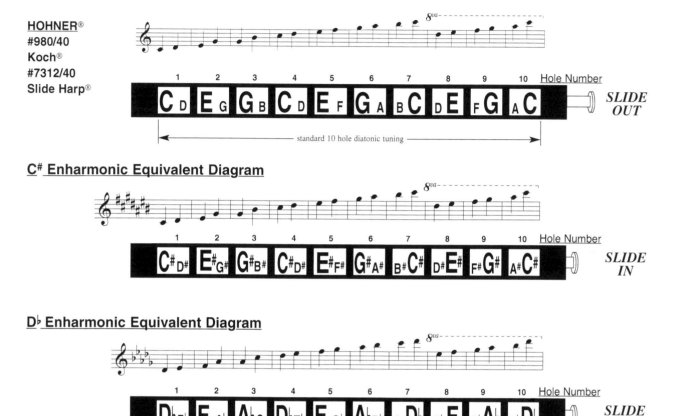

Steve Baker Special®

Hohner's Steve Baker Special® (SBS) model is formatted like a standard 10-hole diatonic, but with three additional holes on the bass end and one added on the high end. The configuration of the notes in the lowest three holes is a duplication of holes 1, 2 and 3 on a standard 10-hole C harp but an octave lower. Hole 1 on the SBS is an octave below middle C. Holes 4 through 13 are the same as a Richter-style C 10-hole major diatonic harp. This model lends itself nicely to bending notes in a range that's an octave lower than the standard 10-hole C harp.

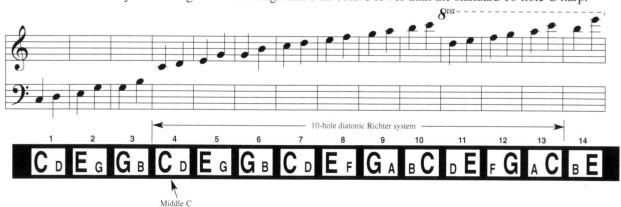

Tremolo-tuned C Diatonic Harmonicas

Many tremolo models are tuned the same as a 10-hole major diatonic harmonicas, except they have separate air channels for the blow and draw notes, giving it, horizontally, 20 holes instead of ten. To achieve the tremolo, an identical row of holes has been added below the upper 20 and a reed is placed in each hole with the same note as the hole above. These additional reeds are tuned slightly sharp of the reed above, causing the tremolo effect. So there are 40 holes (20 above, 20 below) in these Richter-style tremolo harmonica models. If you treat each set of four holes (two below and two above) as one hole on a 10-hole diatonic harmonica, the charts throughout the book will work for these 40-reed models. Because of the way tremolo harmonicas are constructed —with one note per hole—you can't bend, overblow or overdraw notes. Tremolo harps will give you a tone that's similar to an organ or an accordion.

HOHNER®
14-hole model
  #2209/28
16-hole model
  #2309/32
  #8362/32 Echo®
20-hole model
  #2409/40 Echo®
  #2416/40
  Golden Melody®

• The notes on the staff for a 10-hole harp are shown in the ascending order they are played – from left to right.

  On tremolo harps, the draw notes occur and are shown to the right of the blow notes.

SEYDEL®
14-hole Sailor
  #20.280
16-hole Shanty
  #20.320

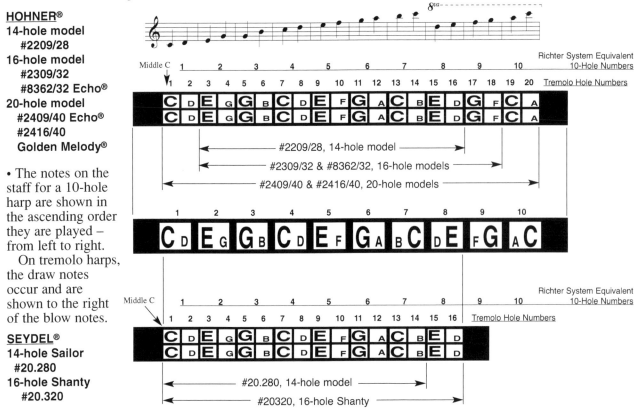

Extended-range Tremolo-tuned C Diatonic Harmonicas

These models are set up the same as the 40-hole tremolo models, except essentially, the first hole has been eliminated and more notes have been added on the high end. The low end starts with the third (E) instead of the root (C) of the key of C. This harp is conducive to playing in 2nd position. Notice the relationship between the additional blow and the draw notes on the upper end of the harp.

HOHNER®
24-hole
  #453/48 Goliath®
  #2509/48 Echo®
  #53/48 Tremolo®

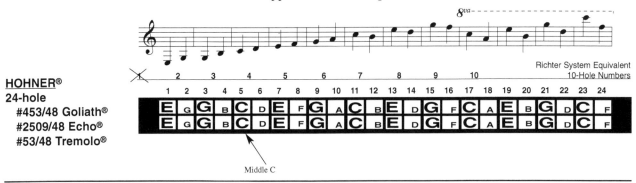

Double-sided Extended-range Tremolo-tuned C Diatonic Harmonicas

HOHNER®
#54/64
#55/80
#56/96 Echo®
#57/120 Echo®
HERING®
Melodiosa®

SEYDEL®
#20.640 Mountain Harp
#21.640 Bergzauber

Double-sided extended-range tremolo-tuned diatonic harmonicas afford a player the widest range of notes. Model 57/120 gives you over four full octaves including an extra E and G. The key of C side of the harp begins on the C below middle C.

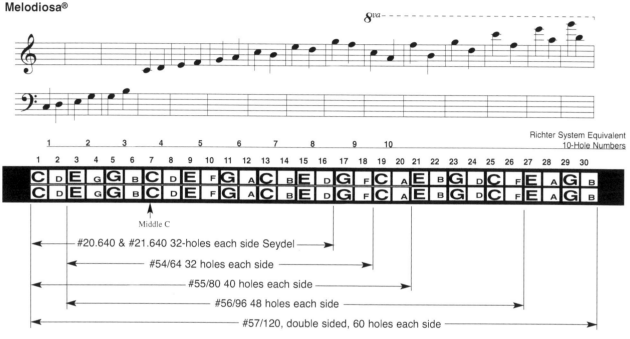

Octave-tuned C Diatonic Harmonicas

TWO NOTES PER HOLE

These models have two notes per hole, horizontally speaking. They are octave-tuned Richter system harps and have 20 holes instead of ten. To get the octaves, the reeds in the lower row are tuned an octave higher than the reeds directly above them. If you treat each set of two holes (one on the bottom and one above) like one hole on the standard 10-hole diatonic harmonica, then the charts in this book apply. There's one exception—in order to bend notes you must play through an individual hole instead of two.

HOHNER®
#105/40
Auto Valve®
#1896/40
CT Marine Band®

SEYDEL®
Concerto Solo®

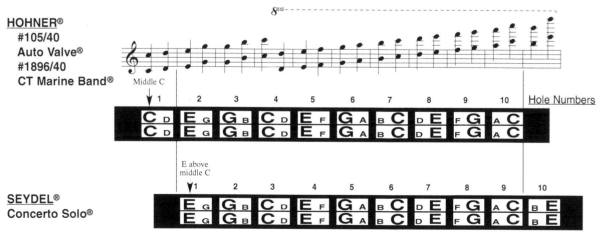

More Octave-tuned C Diatonic Harmonicas

ONE NOTE PER HOLE

These octave-tuned harmonicas also have the same basic tuning as the 10-hole C major diatonic, with two exceptions. First: they have one reed per hole. This equates to 40 holes instead of 10. If you treat each set of four holes (two on the bottom and two above) like one hole on the diatonic harmonica, then the charts in this book for the 10-hole diatonic harmonica will apply. Second: these models are also different in that the first hole "blow" is the 3rd degree of the major scale instead of the root. Think of it as if the first hole of a 10-hole diatonic harp was simply lopped off and the harp starts at the second hole of Richter system. Notice the location of middle C: Even though the notes seem to be out of ascending order towards the upper end, don't fret. Treat, for example, holes 17 and 18 as if they were one hole—hole 10 on a 10-hole diatonic. If you get a little out of sync on the holes (like playing holes 16 and 17), you'll probably notice it and make the necessary adjustment. Due to the way octave harmonicas are constructed, you can't bend or overbend notes.

HOHNER®
14 hole models
  #1494/28
16 hole models
  #1493/32
  #2503/32
20 hole models
  #1495/40
  #2504/40
  #3427/80
HERING®
16 hole models
  #7940 Seductora
  #8332 Sonhadora

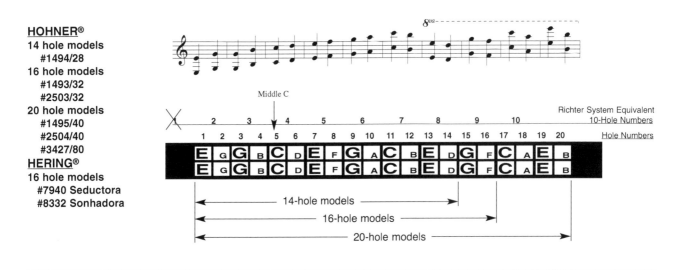

Double-sided C Octave-tuned Extended-range

ONE NOTE PER HOLE

This octave-tuned harmonica has the same design as the 40 hole harps, except four notes have been added (eight holes) on the high end. This model, like the other "one hole per reed" octave harps, begins on the 3rd degree of the C major scale. Treat each set of four holes the same as one hole on the 10-hole diatonic.

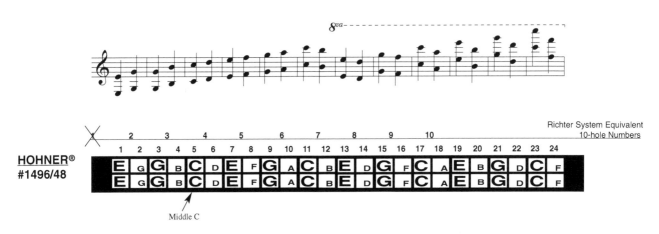

HOHNER®
#1496/48

How the Air Flows

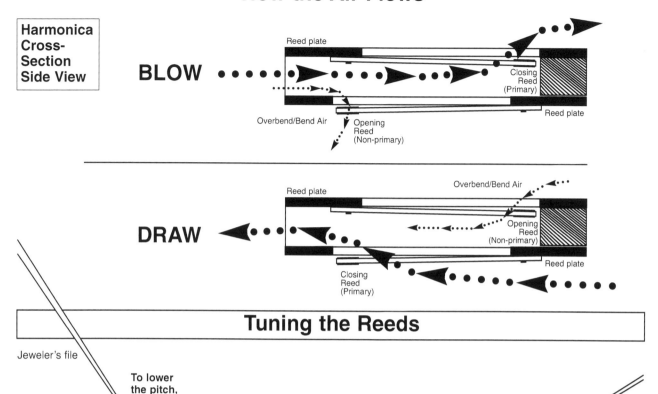

Harmonica Cross-Section Side View

BLOW

Reed plate

Closing Reed (Primary)

Reed plate

Overbend/Bend Air

Opening Reed (Non-primary)

DRAW

Reed plate

Overbend/Bend Air

Opening Reed (Non-primary)

Reed plate

Closing Reed (Primary)

Tuning the Reeds

Jeweler's file

To lower the pitch, file here.

Jeweler's file

razor blade

REED PLATE

feeler gauge

To raise the pitch, file here.

Remove the cover plate. Insert a thin piece of metal under the reed to stabilize it. Either a razor blade or a feeler gauge used for gapping spark plugs will work. With a pointed jeweler's file, remove specks of brass from the reed until the desired pitch is achieved. To sharpen a note, file the reed at about a 45° angle on the end that vibrates, farthest from the rivet. To flatten a pitch, file the brass close to the rivet, along the centerline. Do this with great care and patience. The blow note reeds are inside the air chamber, so you'll need to insert a small screwdriver into the hole and gently push the reed outside the reed plate and slide the thin piece of metal between the reed and reed plate to stabilize it. Use the same technique to sharpen or flatten the pitch of any reed on either reed plate.

Adjusting the Reed Clearance

For Overbending The reeds typically need to be closer to the reed plate than the way they are set at the factory. Push the draw reeds closer with your fingernail and, for the blow reeds, insert a small screwdriver into the air chamber and push the reed up until it remains closer to the reed plate when at rest. If you push the reed too far, it won't play the normal note and will only play the overbend note. If you're not planning on playing overbends, there is probably no need to adjust the reeds.

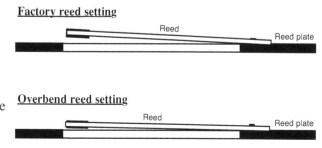

Factory reed setting

Reed

Reed plate

Overbend reed setting

Reed

Reed plate

Glossary

8va: indicates notes are to be played an octave higher than they are written.

10-hole Diatonic Harp: a harmonica with a system of notes based on the Richter system.

12-tone Scale: the chromatic scale made from 12 half steps.

Air Channel: the area in the comb or body of a harmonica through which air passes.

Arpeggio: a chord, typically played ascending one note at a time; a chord played melodically as opposed to harmonically.

Ascending: a note or notes played higher than the previous note(s).

Bar: a vertical line that separates measures; a measure.

Beam: a thick solid line connecting the stems of notes where time values are less than a 1/4 note.

Bend: the act of playing a note lower than the reed note, by constricting or otherwise manipulating the flow of air across the reeds. (See page 10.)

Bent: a note that you must bend to before sounding it; pre-bent.

Blow Chord: a chord played by exhaling.

Blow Note: a single note created by exhaling.

Blue Note: the ♭3, ♭5 or ♭7 degree of the major scale. Also a tone between one of the 12 chromatic notes indicated by a ~ symbol.

Chord: three or more notes played at the same time.

Chromatic: consecutive half steps.

Circle of 5ths: a mathematical musical anomaly that repeats itself (or comes full circle) when you continuously play consecutive ascending fifths.

Closing Reed: when air pressure causes a reed to initially move towards the reed plate, it's called a closing reed.

Comb: the body of a harmonica; the part the reed and cover plates are connected to that defines the air channels.

Descending: playing a pitch lower than the previous one.

Diatonic: referring to a seven-note scale with each of the notes in the musical alphabet included; e.g., C, D, E, F, G, A and B.

Diatonic Harmonica: a harmonica based on the Richter system.

Diminished Triad: a three-note chord built with consecutive ♭3rds.

Draw Chord: a chord that is sounded by inhaling or drawing air through the harmonica and into your lungs.

Draw Note: a note created when you inhale.

Dyad: two notes played at the same time; an interval.

Eighth Note: in this book it represents a bend or overbend note; in standard notation, an eighth the time value of a whole note.

Enharmonic: defines a note or scale with two names—flat and sharp; e.g., E♭ and D♯ sound the same.

Flat: (♭) designates a note 1/2 step lower than the next higher on the chromatic scale; diminished.

Grace Note: in this book, a smaller 1/8 note tied to a 1/4 note shows that more than one note is played on a reed; in standard music notation it's an optional note.

Half Step: (1/2) the smallest unit of the Western scale.

Harmonica: a fixed-reed, mouth-blown musical instrument; also known as mouth organ, harp, Mississippi saxophone, mundharmonika, mund-aeoline, aura, æolina, tin sandwich.

Harp: a harmonica.

Head Shake: playing a rapid succession of notes by holding the harmonica steady and shaking your head.

Hole: the end of an air channel in the comb.

Interval: the musical distance between any two notes; two notes.

Inversion: a chord or scale not in the root position.

Key: defines the relationship of a group of pitches.

Key Signature: the number of sharps or flats at the beginning of a staff or measure indicating the key of the music that follows.

Legato: notes played smoothly from one to the other; a bend.

Major Diatonic Scale: a seven-tone scale; do, re, mi, fa, sol, la, ti, do; intervals: w, w, 1/2, w, w, w, 1/2.

Major Pentatonic Scale: a five-note scale (root, 2, 3, 5, 6).

Minor Pentatonic Scale: a five-note scale (root, ♭3, 4, 5, ♭7).

Mode: the name of the mode and the pattern in which the whole and half steps occur, determined by the degree of the major scale on which the mode begins. (See chart on page 13.)

Natural: (♮) neither sharp nor flat.

Non-primary Reed: the reed other than the main reed intended to be played; e.g., when referring to a note blown on a blow reed, the non-primary reed is the draw reed; when referring to the note drawn on a draw reed, the non-primary reed is the blow reed.

Note: a musical tone; a stable pitch.

Octave: notes that are 12 half steps apart; e.g., C to C or fa to fa.

Opening Reed: when air pressure initially causes a reed to move away from the reed plate, it's called an opening reed.

Overbending: overblowing and overdrawing. (See page 11.)

Pentatonic Scale: a five note scale.

Perfect 5th: (V) a fifth; notes that are five diatonic steps apart; chromatically, 3-1/2 steps apart.

Perfect 4th: (IV) a fourth; an interval of 2-1/2 steps.

Pitch: a stable vibration or musical tone.

Positions: harp players' term for modal playing. (See page 13.)

Pre-bent: a lower note than the reed note that must be played in a bent position initially without playing another note first; bent.

Primary Reed: Either the blow reed or the draw reed being sounded without bending or overbending; when blowing—the blow reed; when drawing—the draw reed.

Quarter Note: in this book, the pitch of a quarter note represents the name of a primary reed; in standard notation, it has a time value that is 1/4 the duration of a whole note.

Reed: a metal strip that vibrates when air passes over it, creating a note or tone.

Reed Note: the note a reed is designed to play; the note you hear when playing a single hole without bending or overbending.

Reed Plate: the plate to which the reeds are attached.

Relative Minor: the minor scale that begins on the sixth degree of any major scale; the relative minor of C is Am.

Richter System: the fixed system of intervals for harmonica developed in 1827 by a man named Richter.

Root: (1) the 1st degree of a scale or chord; the lowest note in a root position chord; tonic.

Root Position: first position; a scale or chord with the 1st degree of the scale as its lowest note.

Scale: a series of notes with fixed intervals.

Scale Degree: the numeric value of ascending diatonic steps beginning at the root. (See page 13.)

Sharp: (♯) designates a note is 1/2 step higher.

Slur: in this book, denotes legato; indicates either two or more bend notes; the connection of a bend or overbend to the reed note; indicates more than one note per reed.

Staccato: a note played briefly and clearly defined from the adjoining note – pre-bent notes may be played staccato.

Staff: the group of five horizontal lines and four spaces where notes appear, establishing their pitch.

Sympathetic Vibration: the vibration of an object that is caused by the vibration of another object.

Tone: a stable pitch; the sound of an instrument.

Tremolo: a continuous slight deviation in volume.

Triad: a three-note chord built with adjacent thirds.

Trills: rapidly alternating tones in succession.

Vibrato: a slight, continuous fluctuation in pitch.

Voicing: playing additional notes in a chord. e.g., G C E G.

Western Music: Western civilization's 12-tone scale and the music derived from it.

Whole Step: (w) two contiguous half steps.

Sources: A Brief History of the Harmonica. M. Hohner Inc. (1975), The New Harvard Dictionary of Music. (1986) Belknap Press of Harvard of Harvard University Press. The Musician's Guide To Harmony and Theory, by Leon White. Professional Music Products. Howard Levy, New Directions For Harmonica, Homespun Tapes. John Sebastian Teaches Blues Harmonica, Homespun Tapes.

Printed in Great Britain
by Amazon.co.uk, Ltd.,
Marston Gate.